DEMCO

TWEED FICTION F

Julia's Kitchen

Julia's Kitchen

~ BRENDA A. FERBER ~

Farrar Straus Giroux / New York

A Note to the Reader

A number of Hebrew and Yiddish terms
appear throughout this story. A glossary
can be found on page 149.

www.fsgkidsbooks.com

Library of Congress Cataloging-in-Publication Data
Ferber, Brenda A.
    Julia's kitchen / Brenda A. Ferber.— 1st ed.
        p. cm.
    Summary: When her mother and younger sister are killed in a house
fire, eleven-year-old Cara struggles to find a way to deal with her
emotions and to reach out to her grieving father.
    ISBN-13: 978-0-374-39932-0
    ISBN-10: 0-374-39932-8
    [1. Grief—Fiction.   2. Fathers and daughters—Fiction.   3. Death—
Fiction.   4. Cookery—Fiction.   5. Fires—Fiction.   6. Jews—United
States—Fiction.]   I. Title.

PZ7.F3543Jul 2006
[Fic]—dc22

                                        2005046921

For Alan, with love

Julia's Kitchen

The last picture I glued into my scrapbook that Sunday morning at Marlee's was of Mom, Dad, Janie, and me at a Cubs game in the summer. I had given my camera to a lady sitting in front of us, and she had snapped a good one. We were all smiling, no one blinked, and you could even see the mustard Janie had dripped on her shirt.

"Cute picture, Cara," Marlee said. We were sprawled on her bedroom floor, surrounded by papers, stickers, markers, and glue.

"Thanks," I said. "Will you help me write 'Go Cubs!' here, but turn the 'o' into a baseball and the exclamation mark into a bat?" Marlee was much more artistic than I was, and I loved her handwriting.

"Sure," Marlee said as she picked up a blue marker.

Just then we heard Marlee's mom call from the kitchen, "Pancakes, hot off the griddle!"

Mrs. Rosen didn't have to ask us twice. We left our scrapbooks and headed into the kitchen, where Marlee's mom served up pancakes shaped like Mickey Mouse heads.

Marlee rolled her eyes and cut the ears off her pancake right away. "She is so embarrassing," Marlee whispered.

I laughed and nodded. Mrs. Rosen's first name was Minnie, and she loved everything Disney. Now that we were eleven, it drove Marlee crazy, but I still thought it was funny.

The phone rang, and Mrs. Rosen picked it up while I smothered my pancake with maple syrup. I was about to pop a bite into my mouth when I heard her gasp.

Marlee and I looked up. Mrs. Rosen turned her back to us. "Oh no," she said into the phone. "Oh . . . no . . ."

The next batch of pancakes started smoking on the griddle. Marlee and I stared at each other. Max, Marlee's twelve-year-old brother, came into the kitchen, wrinkled his nose, and said, "What's burning?"

"Shh!" Marlee and I both said at once. We pointed with our eyes toward Mrs. Rosen, who turned off the electric griddle but left the pancakes smoldering while she continued her phone conversation. She kept saying

"Yes," "I see," and "Oh no." Then she said, "I'm so sorry, David."

That was when my stomach dropped. David was my dad.

Mrs. Rosen hung up the phone and slowly scraped the pancakes into the sink. The room became silent. The smell of burnt pancakes filled the air. Ten loud seconds ticked by on the Alice in Wonderland kitchen clock.

Then Mrs. Rosen turned and walked toward me. She sat down and touched my hand. "Cara, honey, that was your dad. He's at the hospital."

"Is he okay?" I asked, my heart racing.

"He's fine," Mrs. Rosen said. She took a deep breath. "But early this morning there was a fire. At your house."

"A fire?"

Mrs. Rosen nodded. "You need to go to the hospital. I'll take you there."

Suddenly I felt sick to my stomach. "What about my mom? And Janie? Are they okay?"

Mrs. Rosen pressed her lips together. "Your dad just wanted me to get you to the hospital, sweetie. I really don't know all the details, but we can be there in five minutes. Okay?"

"I'm coming, too," Marlee said.

"No," Mrs. Rosen said. "You'll stay here."

I dressed quickly and got into Mrs. Rosen's minivan,

and we headed to Walden Hospital. Even in my winter coat, hat, and gloves, I couldn't stop shaking. Mrs. Rosen tapped her fingers on the steering wheel as we drove.

I pictured Janie, just eight years old, and my mom in hospital beds hooked up to tubes and machines. I concentrated on that picture. I imagined it floating up to God and poking him in his side. *Take care of them*, I thought.

I was used to picturing disasters. I did it a lot. Once, Mom and Dad went to a friend's wedding in San Diego, and Janie and I had to stay with Nana and Papa in Chicago. Even though we lived just a few suburbs away from them, they were not our favorite grandparents. I wondered what might happen if Mom and Dad didn't come back. Would we be stuck with Nana and Papa forever? All weekend long I imagined our parents' plane crashing or their hotel blowing up. When they finally got home safely, I felt so grateful. And, in a way, powerful. It was as if my worries had acted like little whispers in God's ear, nudging him into action.

It worked so well that I tried it again. And again. And again. Every time I worried, things turned out fine. I figured I was God's helper. I worried, and he swooped in to take care of everything. In the last couple of years I'd prevented hundreds of car crashes, kidnappings, and murders with my morbid imagination.

I had to admit, though, this time was different. This time the bad thing had already happened. I'd never thought to worry about a fire. So now I could only wonder if God had been there, helping. *Please, God, tell me you helped my family this morning*, I prayed.

But my gut told me Mom and Janie were not okay. Mrs. Rosen would have said so if they were. Or she would have turned on the radio, or made small talk, or something. Instead, she just kept glancing at me with a face full of concern, saying nothing at all.

I stared out the window at the morning light. The sun reflected off the freshly fallen snow, making it so bright it hurt my eyes. How different from the gray January days we'd been having. Maybe God was giving me a sign. Maybe everything would be okay. I took a deep breath and told myself to calm down. Everything would be fine. It had to be.

~ ~ ~

My legs wobbled as we rushed into the emergency waiting room and looked around. There were two firefighters talking to an old man who was slumped in a chair with his face in his hands. He lifted his head, and I stopped in my tracks. It was Dad. His hair looked gray instead of brown. His eyes were red and puffy. His whole face looked older, like Papa's.

"Dad," I said, running into his arms, "what happened?"

Dad held me close. He smelled like smoke. My stomach tightened. He didn't say anything for a minute. Then in a gravelly voice he mumbled into my hair, "There was a fire. A big fire."

I pulled away. "I know, I know. But where are Mom and Janie? Can I see them?"

The taller firefighter touched Dad's shoulder. "Mr. Segal," he said, "we can finish this later. Take your time with your daughter." He walked away with the other firefighter and Mrs. Rosen. Dad and I were left alone in the waiting room.

"Cara," he said softly, "I don't know how to . . . I'm sorry, I . . ." He sighed and looked at the floor.

I could barely breathe. "What?" I demanded. "Tell me."

Dad held both my hands and looked straight at me. "Mom and Janie didn't make it, Cara. They didn't make it out of the house."

My heart stopped.

I felt as if I were falling through the floor. I shook my head—*no, no, no*—and searched Dad's face for something that would make sense. "What do you mean?" I said. "What happened?"

He ran his hands through his hair. "They brought them here. They tried to save them. But they . . . I'm sorry, Cara. It was too late."

"What do you mean?" I repeated, my voice growing stronger. "That can't be right!" The room started spinning, and I thought I was going to throw up. I pounded my fists against his chest. "Please, Daddy, tell me it's not true!"

I heard a buzzing in my ears, and then a high-pitched wail. A nurse came over and said, "Shh, honey, shh, it's all right," and then I realized I was the one making that sound. But I couldn't stop.

I felt Dad's arms around me. Mom and Janie couldn't really be dead, I thought. I just saw them yesterday. *Where were you, God? Where were you when my house was burning?*

~ ~ ~

Mrs. Rosen drove us the thirty minutes from the hospital to Nana and Papa's apartment in Chicago. When we walked in, my grandparents hugged me, but I didn't hug them back. I just stood there, staring at their orange shag carpeting, wondering how these old boring people could be alive if Mom and Janie were dead.

The apartment smelled like cooked broccoli, and Dad still smelled like smoke, and the two smells combined to make me nauseous. I went straight to the only comfortable place to sit—an oversized green chair that felt like velvet. Janie and I used to fight over that seat all the time.

She'd yell, "I call the chair," as soon as we stepped through the front door. Then I'd say, "No calling," and beat her to the spot, sprawling out in it.

But now as I curled up in the chair, it seemed so big. Big enough to share.

I pretended there was a magic wall around me. I could see out, but nobody could see in. I became small. I became invisible.

Everyone whispered. They whispered about the fire, the hospital, and the funeral arrangements. No TV, no radio—just whispers interrupted by the telephone. Whenever it rang, I imagined Mom was calling to say she'd be over as soon as she picked up Janie from soccer or something. Marlee called, but I didn't want to talk to her. I didn't want to talk to anyone. I didn't want to think. I didn't want to breathe. I just wanted Mom and Janie.

That's how the first day passed.

~ ~ ~

The next day was Monday, a school day. I didn't go. I took my spot on the green chair first thing in the morning and picked at my nails. I realized I hadn't eaten since Saturday night or said a word to anyone since we left the hospital. Nana had made me drink some water, but it had tasted bad, like stale ice. A nagging question kept running through my head: How did Dad get out of the house without Mom and Janie? I wanted to ask him, but I couldn't. Dad seemed like a different person, like a faded photograph of himself.

I thought of all my photographs, all my scrapbooks, lost in the fire. I was left with only the one scrapbook and the box of supplies I'd taken to Marlee's.

Some friends of Nana and Papa's and a few people from our synagogue came by, including Rabbi Newlin. They brought casseroles and coffee cakes. Dad shook their hands and nodded politely from his seat next to the phone. I pretended to sleep behind my magic wall so they wouldn't talk to me. All the while I thought about Mom and Janie.

I saw Janie wearing her Cubs hat and throwing a ball in the air. I saw her playing soccer and running faster than any of the kids in her class, even faster than Justin Wittenberg, her best friend. I saw her sitting with Dad, watching sports on TV. I saw her leaning in the doorway of my room. Usually I'd tell her to get out, quit pestering me. But if I had nothing to do, I'd invite her in and she would look through my scrapbooks and laugh at my captions, and I'd feel cool.

I saw Mom in the kitchen, her curly brown hair pulled back in a ponytail like mine. I saw her cheeks smudged with flour or chocolate. A smile on her face. Baking. Always baking. Last year, after her cookies sold out faster than anything else at my school's Valentine's Day bake sale, she started her own business, Julia's Kitchen. She made gift baskets filled with her cookies and brownies. I helped whenever I could. She said I was her official egg-cracker and her unofficial spoon-licker.

They had to be alive. This had to be a mistake.

In the afternoon Dad and Papa went to the house to meet with the fire inspector and the man from the insurance agency. I wanted to go with them. I wanted to see our house with my own eyes. I even got up from my chair and silently put on my coat when I saw them getting ready to go. But Nana took the coat away and said, "No, David, she doesn't need to see."

And Dad believed her.

The funeral would be tomorrow. Everything was happening too fast.

"Eat," Nana said, coming over to offer me a turkey sandwich. "You'll feel better if you eat, Cara, darling."

I pushed her hand away.

Nana set the plate on the coffee table and sighed. Then she sat down next to me.

I wondered what she knew about the fire. She and Dad had stayed up late last night. Maybe Dad had talked to her. Maybe she'd be able to explain it to me. I'd have to break out from behind the magic wall to find out. I'd have to speak an actual sentence. In my head I practiced. *Nana, may I ask you something? Nana, may I ask you something?* Then I cleared my throat and tried out my voice. "Nana?

May I ask you something?" I sounded surprisingly normal.

"Of course, darling."

I swallowed hard. "How did Dad get out of the house
without Mom and Janie?"

Nana frowned and straightened her back. "What kind
of a question is that?" she asked.

"I don't know," I said, feeling suddenly as if I had done
something wrong. "I just can't imagine how it all happened. I mean, why is he alive and they're not?"

"What, you think he didn't try to save them?" Nana's
bony face twisted in anger. "Believe me, he tried. It's a
miracle you're not an orphan."

"That's not what I meant, Nana," I said, blinking back
tears.

"Well, that's how it sounded."

"I'm sorry, I just . . ." I didn't finish my sentence. I
didn't know what to say. How could I expect Nana to
understand? She never listened to me.

"Why don't you eat, Cara?" she said again, pushing the
plate my way.

I decided to stay behind my magic wall forever.

~ ~ ~

Later, when Dad and Papa returned, Bubbe and
Zayde, Mom's parents, who lived in Florida, arrived with

them. Bubbe dropped her small suitcase in the foyer and headed straight for me. She wasn't wearing any makeup. Her face looked pale, her skin papery thin. And her hazel eyes, so much like Mom's, were somehow different now, heavy. She sat on the edge of the chair, took my hands in hers, and looked at me without saying a word.

Those familiar eyes, speckled with green, yellow, and brown, reached me right through my magic wall. I knew for sure then, knew it with my whole body, that Mom and Janie were really dead. I buried my face in Bubbe's neck.

"I know," she said between my sobs. "Let it out, love, let it out. I'm here."

Zayde put his arms around us both, and we cried and rocked together until our sweaters were soaked with tears.

I stayed glued to Bubbe and Zayde the rest of the day. Bubbe rubbed my back, and Zayde told me stories from when Mom was little: about the time Mom threw up all over the stage in the middle of her second-grade concert, and the time she ran away from home to protest being an only child. I'd heard all the stories before, but I listened as if they were new.

"I remember when your mom first brought your dad home to meet us," Zayde said. "Remember, David?"

We looked at Dad. He blinked and shook his head, as though trying to wake up from a bad dream. Then he stood and left the room. Just like that.

My heart thunked against my ribs. How could it beat when it was breaking in pieces?

Bubbe patted my hand and said quietly, "It's hardest for him, love. He was there."

But I thought it was hardest for me. Because I wasn't.

At six o'clock the Rosens came by with some clothes for me and dinner from Mario's—pasta and salad. Mrs. Rosen and Nana headed to the kitchen, and Mr. Rosen sat with Bubbe, Zayde, and Papa around Papa's card table. Dad was in the den, napping or hiding, I wasn't sure which. Marlee squeezed in with me on the green chair, and Max sat on the sofa next to us. Marlee put her arm around me. I could tell by her eyes that she'd been crying. And she had the hiccups. Marlee always got the hiccups when she cried.

She said, "I can't believe it, Cara. It's so weird." Then she hiccuped real loud. She slapped her hand over her mouth, embarrassed.

Max shook his head at her. "Jeez, Marlee. Hold your breath or something."

Marlee plugged her nose and puffed her cheeks out. Her face turned as red as her hair, and her freckles practically popped off her cheeks. Now she was hiccuping big, silent hiccups.

The next thing I knew, I was laughing. Marlee let the air out of her cheeks, and she started laughing, too, and everyone in the room looked at us as if we were crazy.

"I'm sorry," Marlee said, trying to control herself.

"It's okay," I said.

And it really was. Because it was bad enough that Mom and Janie were dead, my house was gone, and Dad had pretty much checked out. At least Marlee was still Marlee.

The Rosens stayed for dinner, and I actually managed to eat. I was relieved when Dad came out of the den and joined us at the table. But then the grownups started talking about work and insurance stuff. Nobody mentioned Mom or Janie or the fire, which seemed awfully strange to me.

"I didn't say goodbye to Janie," I said to no one in particular. Everyone turned and looked at me.

"I mean, when Mrs. Rosen picked me up, I said goodbye to Mom. She kissed me and said she loved me. But then I just left."

Bubbe put her arm around me, and I rested my head on her shoulder. "Oh, love," she said. "There was no way for you to know."

"But I don't even remember our last conversation. Janie was playing Monopoly with Dad. Maybe I said something stupid like don't buy Water Works." I pictured Janie rolling the dice. She was the race car, her favorite piece. Janie's cat, Sport, was swatting a couple of the plastic houses at Janie's feet.

Sport! How could I have forgotten Sport?

"What happened to Sport?" I asked.

Nobody said anything. Dad looked at his plate.

"Is Sport dead, too?" I felt my blood rush. "Is he?" I pushed away from the table and stood next to Dad.

He looked up, his eyes filled with tears.

"How could they all die?" I yelled. Then I stormed out of the room, not even caring what the Rosens or my grandparents thought.

I slammed the door to the spare bedroom and flung myself on the bed. I got up and paced the room. Threw pillows on the floor. Kicked the dresser.

Dad knocked on the door and opened it at the same time. I hated that.

"Go away!" I screamed.

He stood in the doorway. His shaggy hair looked shaggier. His whole body sagged. "Cara," he said. "Please."

I turned away, breathing hard. He put his hand on my shoulder, but I shook him off. A moment later he left, closing the door behind him.

I fell onto the bed and curled up in a ball. I waited and waited for Mom to come in and tell me everything would be okay. Even though I knew she couldn't come, I waited.

~ two ~

The next day, at the funeral home, the funeral director took us into a small room to wait until the service began. Rabbi Newlin came in. He shook hands with everyone and explained that it was time for keriah.

"What's that?" I asked.

"Traditionally, keriah is when mourners tear their clothing to signify their loss. But today, instead of tearing their clothes, many Jews wear a black ribbon like this one." He showed me a piece of black ribbon about the size of two of my fingers put together. "According to Jewish law, your father and your Bubbe and Zayde are the only official mourners here. Since you're not yet twelve years old, Cara, you're not obligated to mourn, but you're a mature girl, almost Bat Mitzvah age. You might want to be counted as a mourner."

Everybody looked at me. I wondered if Mom and Janie were looking at me from heaven. I didn't know I'd have a choice about mourning.

"Okay," I said.

All my grandparents nodded in approval. Dad ran his hands through his hair, then looked at the floor.

"Well, then," said Rabbi Newlin, gesturing for us to stand. "Let's begin."

Rabbi Newlin pinned the ribbon on the right-hand side of Zayde's shirt. Then he made a small tear in the ribbon. Bubbe gripped Zayde's arm, and they held on to each other, their faces wrinkled with sadness. The rabbi did the same thing to Bubbe and Dad. But for me, he pinned the ribbon on my left side.

"When you mourn a parent, you honor her by making the rip near your heart," he explained softly as he tore my ribbon.

The black ribbon looked out of place against the blue dress Mrs. Rosen had bought me. But the tear in it matched my feelings. I knew my heart was torn.

We left the small waiting room and walked into the front of the chapel. There were hundreds of people there. I saw kids from school. People from ADF Advertising, where Dad worked. Tons of friends and relatives. And people I didn't even recognize. We took our seats in the first row, and I felt everyone's eyes on me. Poor Cara, they were probably thinking, and they were right.

I didn't know where to look. Right in front of me were two caskets, one big and one small. I couldn't believe Mom and Janie were really in those wooden boxes with the lids shut tight. Mom was terrified of being stuck in small spaces. I started to feel that I couldn't breathe. My tongue felt too big for my mouth, as if it were choking me. I looked down and picked at my nails. There was almost nothing left to pick.

I looked up again, avoiding the caskets. I reminded myself that only Mom's and Janie's bodies were inside. Their spirits were free. I gazed across the room and found a small window. Through the window I saw blue sky and tree branches.

I imagined Mom as a floating spirit, an angel flitting about. She held Janie's hand and pointed out all the people. Janie wore a party hat, and Mom had a lei around her neck and a flowery wreath on her head. Platters of cake and ice cream appeared before them. Their faces glowed with joy. It was as if Mom had planned the biggest birthday party ever.

Was that heaven? I wasn't sure, but it was definitely better to think of Mom and Janie that way than stuck inside those caskets. I took a deep breath and focused on this imaginary birthday party as Rabbi Newlin started the service.

"My friends, let us begin by reciting a psalm that expresses the intimate relationship between God and man. When trouble abounds, when agony strikes the soul, we are comforted by our faith in God . . ."

Faith in God? Where was the comfort in that? I had faith in God, and look what happened. God deserted me. He deserted my family.

Rabbi Newlin's slow, hypnotic voice melted into a rhythmic sort of chant. Was he even speaking English? I tuned him out and concentrated instead on the birthday party scene in my mind.

Time passed. Maybe a few minutes. Maybe more. It didn't matter. But I became aware of the funeral again as Rabbi Newlin called on people to give eulogies. First Mr. Wittenberg, Justin's dad, spoke. He talked about what a talented athlete Janie had been, and what a good friend. I hadn't thought much about Justin during all of this. What would he do without Janie? They had been as close as Marlee and I were.

Next up was Mom's best friend from college, Roz Tallman. Roz was an actress in Hollywood. Actually, she worked as a receptionist at a talent agency. She had been in only two movies, and Mom and Dad hadn't let me see either of them. But still, Roz had stage presence. She stood at the podium, her shiny blond hair framing her perfectly madeup face. She wore a leopard print blouse and a short black leather skirt. What an outfit! I wondered if Mom and Janie were laughing about her clothes. I wished Janie were sitting next to me. I would elbow her, and we would both try not to laugh.

"Julia loved to bake," Roz was saying. "But more important, she loved to share her baking with others. I can't tell you the number of times I received packages in the mail filled with her fresh-baked cookies. Just like her gift baskets for her business, every container included an inspirational note: 'Reach for the stars,' or 'Don't give up,' or 'Smile, you're in California.' You see, Julia had a natural way of loving and giving to people."

Roz dabbed at her eyes with a tissue. She looked out at everyone and took a deep breath. "And she loved her family more than anything. Which is why I can understand what she did. Julia wouldn't have had to think twice about running into that burning house to save her daughter."

Roz kept talking, but I didn't hear anything after that. Goose bumps prickled my arms. My stomach flipped. Mom ran into the house? That meant she had gotten out. Why hadn't anyone told me that? I turned to Dad, but he kept staring straight ahead. Mom had escaped and then deliberately run back in. How could she do that to me? Where were the firefighters? And where was Dad? He could have stopped her. I would have stopped her. Or maybe I would have helped Janie get out in the first place.

Oh, why hadn't I been there? Why had I slept at Marlee's that night? If only I'd been home. If only I'd thought to worry about a fire. I was always worrying about something. Why hadn't I worried about a fire? Maybe if I had, God would have heard me, and it never would have happened.

Why pounded in my head for the rest of the funeral. It pounded as we recited kaddish, the prayer for mourners. It pounded as the caskets were lowered down, down, down into the cold ground. *Why* pounded as we each shoveled three scoops of dirt into the graves. And it pounded as people murmured words of comfort to my family. Words that meant nothing to me. Nobody could tell me *why*.

~ ~ ~

Back at Nana and Papa's apartment, Zayde lit two big candles in glass jars that would burn the whole seven days of shiva, the first mourning period. Someone had covered all the mirrors in the apartment with sheets, and had put pillows on the floor and set out plastic seats that looked like lawn chairs with their legs cut in half. Zayde told me that sitting low on one of those chairs or on the floor symbolized our sadness. We weren't allowed to get any food for ourselves or help with the dishes or anything.

Friends and relatives did it all. We didn't have to greet anyone or say thank you either. I liked those customs.

I sat on a pillow in a corner of the living room. Marlee brought me a hard-boiled egg on a paper plate.

"My mom says you're supposed to eat this," she said.

I wrinkled my nose. I didn't like hard-boiled eggs.

"Eat it," Marlee said. "It's symbolic of life."

I took a small bite. It wasn't so bad.

We watched the room fill with people. It seemed that everyone I'd ever known came to Nana and Papa's that afternoon. The apartment was hot and noisy.

Mrs. Olsen, our gray-haired next-door neighbor, brought me a bagel with lox and cream cheese. She perched on a chair next to Marlee and me and shook her head. "It's such a shame," she said. "Such wonderful people."

"Thank you," I said.

"We don't always understand God's reasons," she said, sipping her coffee. "But at least your mom and Janie are at peace. They're in a better place now."

I nodded politely and bit into the bagel. But inside I cringed. A better place? Better than with Dad and me? All day long, people kept saying these things: "God works in mysterious ways," or "God must have needed them in heaven." Every mention of God made me tense. I used to think God was my partner. But what kind of partner would let this happen?

Roz came over with a piece of noodle kugel. "How're you doing, honey?" she asked.

I shrugged. We didn't say anything for a minute, and I nibbled at the sweet kugel. Then I looked at Roz and said, "I didn't know Mom ran back into the house to save Janie."

Roz raised her tweezed eyebrows in surprise. "No? You didn't see the articles in the paper?"

I shook my head.

"And your father didn't talk to you?"

I shook my head again.

"Oh, sweetheart, I'm so sorry." Roz rubbed my shoulder. "Give your dad time. He'll come around."

I glanced at Dad, sitting in one of the low chairs on the other side of the living room. He didn't look anything like himself, in Papa's suit, his hair going in every direction.

"Why don't you just talk to him?" Marlee asked.

"I can't," I said.

Part of me wanted to shake Dad, punch him, yell at him for letting Mom and Janie die. But another part wanted to hug him and have him tell me everything would be all right.

"What else do you know?" I asked Roz. "About the fire."

Roz uncrossed, then crossed her legs again. "Well, the article today said it started in the kitchen. From an electrical short in the toaster oven, of all things."

"The toaster oven?" Marlee and I both said at the same time.

Roz nodded. "I guess you're supposed to unplug it when you're not using it. But you should pull it out by the plug, never the cord."

"Well, ours was always plugged in," I said.

"I know, honey," Roz said, patting my hand. "Mine, too. But not anymore. You run the risk of accidentally leaving it on, or a wire shorting out, or who knows what else."

"Jeez," Marlee said. "You'd think they'd tell you all that during Fire Safety Week at school!"

I sat there, imagining a spark from our toaster oven lighting—what? A kitchen towel? The curtains? Had I left a napkin out on the counter, next to the toaster oven? Was that how the fire had spread? I pushed the kugel away from me.

Max came over carrying a plate piled high with brownies and coffee cake. Chocolate crumbs edged the corner of his mouth. "Dessert!" he announced.

Marlee rolled her eyes. "You pig."

"Excuse me!" he said. "I brought these to share." He held the plate in front of me. "Want some?"

The sweet smell of chocolate made my stomach turn, and I felt the egg, the bagel, and the kugel bubble inside me. "No," I said. "No desserts." Then I escaped to the bathroom.

I wished I could cover my brain the way they covered the mirrors. Just shut everything down and quiet my mind. Everyone was trying to comfort me, but I didn't want comfort. I wanted Mom and Janie. And those desserts were the worst of it. *Your mom is gone and she'll never bake with you again.* Well, I knew one thing for sure. I would never eat another dessert. Never.

~ ~ ~

That night, when everyone finally left, I got ready for bed. I put on pajamas, brushed my teeth, and crawled underneath Nana's flowery bedspread in the guest room. I lay in the dark, thinking about Mom and Janie. I wished Mom could kiss me good night just one more time. I wished Janie could sneak into my room for one more silly knock-knock joke. Or one more peek at my scrapbooks.

I thought about Dad, sleeping on the pull-out sofa in the den. We hadn't spoken to each other since yesterday. I was scared to hear what he'd have to say, but at the same time I wanted to talk to him so badly. I tiptoed out of the guest room. I didn't want to wake Nana and Papa. I needed Dad to myself. I needed to know what happened the morning of the fire. I needed to know everything.

As I tiptoed down the hall, I imagined the conversation Dad and I would have. I'd say, Daddy, I'm so sorry I wasn't there to help. Please, tell me what happened. And he'd say, It was terrible, Cara. And then he'd tell me every detail, and we'd hug and promise to take care of each other and to never leave the toaster oven plugged in again.

But as I got closer to the end of the hall, I heard the sound of muffled sobs. I took two tiny steps forward and cracked open the door to the den. In the moonlit room I saw Dad, huddled on the bed, crying into a pillow.

I stood, frozen. I had never seen him cry before. Even at the funeral, his eyes got all watery, but he didn't cry. Watching him now made my own eyes fill with tears. My legs started to shake. I didn't know what to do. I knew Dad wouldn't want me to see him that way. So I backed away from the door. I hurried into bed and hugged my knees to my chest. I squeezed my eyes shut and tried to erase the picture of Dad crying like that. But it burned into the back of my eyelids.

~ three ~

Wednesday morning, when there were no visitors, Bubbe and I sat in the living room while Dad, Zayde, Nana, and Papa ate breakfast in the kitchen. Bubbe took out her sketchpad and colored pencils. "Turn on that lamp next to you, love," she said.

I did as Bubbe asked, then settled back in the green chair. "You're not going to draw me, are you?"

"Why not?" She had already started sketching. Her eyes darted from the paper to me, and back again.

"I look ugly. That's why. I haven't even seen a mirror since yesterday morning."

"Don't be ridiculous. You're beautiful." Bubbe paused, gazing at me. "You look just like your mother."

We smiled at each other then. But they weren't regular smiles. They were smiles tinged with sadness.

Bubbe's pencils made a soft scratching sound. The refrigerator hummed. The apartment smelled like coffee. "Bubbe?" I asked.

"Yes, love?"

"What's going to happen to me?"

Bubbe looked up from her drawing and met my eyes. She studied me for a moment. "You're going to be okay, Cara. We'll all be okay eventually."

"But, Bubbe, Dad is different now," I whispered. "I feel like I don't even know him."

Bubbe sighed. "I know, love. But he's your father. And he's a good man. We just have to give him some time. Right now I think he's still in shock."

"Well, so am I."

Bubbe frowned, but her eyes smiled. She patted the seat next to her. "Come here." I snuggled next to her and watched as she finished the drawing. "I suppose we're all in shock now," she said, adding different shades of brown to my hair and eyes. "We have to take care of each other." She signed her name to the bottom of the picture, dated it, and handed it to me. "Now, is that an ugly girl?" she asked.

There I was, the same Cara as before. Curly hair pulled back in a ponytail. Brown eyes and dark curly lashes. Long nose, long chin, long neck. It was Mom's face. Everyone said so. I looked like Mom, and Janie looked like Dad. It was fair that way. We each had our match. And not just in appearance, but in personality, too. Dad and Janie were the ones who rode the rickety roller coasters while Mom and I ate cotton candy and took in a show. And Mom and I were the ones who cheered from the sidelines while Janie played soccer and Dad coached. Mom and I were sensible, quiet, maybe even a little boring. If not for Marlee, I'd say Mom had been my best friend.

I gave the picture back to Bubbe. "It's good," I said. "You should keep it."

~ ~ ~

Shiva turned into a haze of naps, deli trays, visiting, and praying. At the prayer services each morning and evening, I pretended to follow along while I daydreamed about Mom and Janie. I found I could say simple things to Dad, such as, "Is there any more coleslaw?" or "The synagogue sure collected a lot of nice clothes for us."

Which they had, thank goodness. Because that first day when Dad had gone to the house, he'd brought back the clothes that had made it through the fire. The only items not damaged by smoke and heat had been in closed dresser drawers. In my case that meant socks and underwear. I guess I'd been in a hurry when I'd packed for Marlee's, and I'd neglected to shut all but one of my drawers. Dad, on the other hand, retrieved most of his sweats and T-shirts and stuff. But I bet he was pretty upset about losing the suits and work clothes that had hung in his closet. Not that he'd say so. Anyway, Dad seemed satisfied with our bits of conversation, and he never once mentioned Mom, Janie, or the fire.

~ ~ ~

Thursday night, as I listened to some people from Dad's ad agency go on and on about their recent trip to Costa Rica, Mrs. Rosen and Marlee walked in carrying my scrapbook box. Marlee smiled and waved at me, then set the big plastic box on the foyer table and took off her coat. The sight of my scrapbook box, something so normal from before the fire, gave me a jolt of energy.

"Excuse me for a minute," I said, and practically ran to greet Marlee.

"Ta-da!" she said, handing me the box.

"Oh, Marlee! Thank you!"

Mrs. Rosen gave me a kiss and asked, "How're you doing, sweetie?"

"Better now," I said, nodding at the box. "Thanks for bringing it . . . and Marlee!"

"Marlee said it'd make your day. I'm so glad."

As Marlee and I headed back to the guest room, where we could go through the scrapbook box in private, she told me, "I found the articles in the paper—both of them—about the fire. They were in our recycle bin. Mom wouldn't let me bring them tonight, but I'm saving them for you."

"Did you read them?"

Marlee nodded.

"Well?"

"They didn't really say anything we don't already know, but . . . well . . . there's a picture. And, I don't know, you'll have to read them. It's weird. They make it seem so real."

Real. Would I ever get used to it?

I had already made a mental list of everything in the scrapbook box. Besides my newest scrapbook and all the stickers, papers, markers, and scissors, I knew there were two envelopes with photos in there—one from Thanksgiving and Hanukkah, and one from our December vacation to Florida.

Marlee and I sat on the bed with the box between us. "Well, come on. Open it," Marlee urged.

I stared at the box. Then I traced my finger around the top. "It's just hard to believe this is all there is."

"I know," Marlee said. Then she tilted her head to the side. "But at least you have this."

That was true. I snapped off the lid and took in a sharp breath. Right on top were two framed photos—one of Mom relaxing on a raft in the ocean and one of Janie standing proudly next to a sandcastle. Tears instantly filled my eyes and spilled out onto my cheeks.

Marlee put her arms around me. "Cara, Cara, I'm so sorry! Don't cry. I thought this would make you happy."

I caught my breath and wiped at my tears. "No, it's okay. I am. I mean, thank you."

We sat there together, looking at the pictures, not saying anything for a minute.

Finally, Marlee said, "There were doubles of these pictures, so I figured it would be okay. My mom helped me frame them."

I felt a huge lump in my throat. "I remember this day." I pointed to the picture of Janie. She was smiling her goofy smile, her tongue squeezing out between her teeth. "Janie and Dad worked on that sandcastle all afternoon. They were so proud of it.

"And this one," I said, looking at the picture of Mom. "I remember squishing in with her on the raft right after I took this."

"Good memories, huh?"

"Yeah. Thanks, Mar." I wiped one last tear from my eye and gave her a hug.

We looked through my scrapbook. It was a new one, and I'd only filled four pages so far. The picture of my family at the Cubs game reminded me of Sunday morning at Marlee's. Marlee had written "Go Cubs!" just the way I'd wanted. But now when I looked at the four of us together, the caption seemed wrong. It should have said "Go Segals!"

I closed the scrapbook and took out the other photographs from the envelopes. There was Mom spreading whipped cream on her pumpkin pie just before I licked the bowl clean. And Janie and Dad putting up the Hanukkah decorations. There was Janie playing in the ocean with Dad. And there was Mom looking at one of my older scrapbooks. I began to see a pattern.

"Marlee, you know how people have been saying God must have a reason for this that we just don't understand?"

"Yeah?"

"Well, what if that's true? What if God actually did this for a reason?"

"No way," Marlee said, scrunching up her round freckled face. "What reason could there be?"

"I don't know," I said. I got up from the bed and propped the framed photos on the dresser. With my back to Marlee I said, "What if maybe God thought I wasn't spending enough time alone with my dad? What if he wanted us to be closer?"

"Cara, what are you talking about?"

I turned around to face Marlee. "I'm just saying, it was always Mom and me, Dad and Janie. Look at the pictures."

Marlee glanced at the photos spread out on the bed. Then she shook her head and looked up at me. "So let me get this straight. You think God started a fire at your house and killed your mom and Janie so that you and your dad could be closer?"

"Is that crazy?"

"Of course it's crazy!" Marlee jumped off the bed and put her hands on my shoulders. She blew her bangs out of her eyes and looked me square in the face. "Cara, the fire was an accident. I don't know why your mom and Janie died. But I am sure that God didn't do it on purpose."

"But then why? Why did it happen?"

"I don't know," Marlee said, shrugging.

"Well, maybe there is no God," I said quietly.

Marlee squinted at me. "What? Cara! Don't say that! He might be listening!"

It was my turn to shrug. "Never mind," I said. "Forget it."

But I was thinking. What if whenever I thought God was watching out for me, I was just having good luck? And now my luck had run out? What if God didn't exist? That would explain the fire, right? The idea sat in the pit of my stomach like a rock, heavy and hard.

~ ~ ~

The next day, I was resting in the guest room. Then all of a sudden, I was coming home from school. The sweet smell of rising bread met me before I even got through the front door. Our front door. Our house. Mom was baking challah, the braided bread we ate at Friday night Shabbat dinners. I dropped my coat and backpack by the front door.

"Hi, hon!" Mom called out. "How was your day?"

I ran back to the kitchen, breathless. Mom stood there, punching down the dough, wearing the "Julia's Kitchen" apron Janie and I had made for her birthday. I couldn't believe it—Mom was alive!

The kitchen was in perfect order, as always. She smiled at me while I stood dumbfounded, staring at her.

"You're just in time to help me braid. Are your hands clean?" Mom took out a knife and began cutting the dough into pieces. I washed my hands, and she passed me a piece of dough.

I rolled the dough between my palms, making a long snake, all the while staring at Mom.

"I got three more orders today, Cara. Can you believe that? I'm telling you, this little business of mine is really taking off." Mom took my snake and handed me a new piece of dough to roll. The late afternoon sun streamed through the window and lit up her face. "You know, I never would have started Julia's Kitchen if you hadn't convinced me. I can't believe people are actually paying me to do what I love."

She looked up from the challah and locked eyes with me. I memorized her face. The angle of her chin. The smile lines by her eyes. The freckle on the side of her nose. "What are you looking at?" she asked.

"Just you."

"Come here, sweetie." Mom took my dough and placed it on the counter. Then she wrapped her arms around me. "I love you, delicious girl."

"I love you, too, Mom."

And then she disappeared. It was a dream. Tears streamed down my cheeks, soaking the pillow. My head throbbed and my heart ached so much it scared me.

I was still at Nana and Papa's. But the smell of challah was so real. I wiped my eyes, then opened the bedroom door and followed the smell into the kitchen. I should have guessed—Bubbe.

"Well, hello, love."

"You're baking challah?"

"Tonight's Shabbat."

"But I thought we weren't allowed to bake during shiva."

"Well, maybe so, but I wanted to bake challah, so that's what I'm doing."

I put my face close to the loaves of braided dough. "It smells like Mom. Bubbe, I just dreamed about her. She was making challah, too. She was so . . . alive."

Bubbe gripped the counter with both hands. Then she let out a long sigh and nodded. She beat an egg and brushed it gently on the braided loaves.

"Did you teach Mom to make challah?"

"Mmm-hmm. Like my mom taught me. This recipe has been in our family for generations."

I thought of all Mom's recipes. Just ashes now. I wished Mom had taught me to bake challah. Not just the braiding and the egg wash, but the whole thing. She usually made the dough while I was at school. I had figured she'd teach me when I got older.

Bubbe read my mind. "I can teach you, Cara. When you're ready."

I looked at Bubbe. Her eyes were oceans.

I loved Bubbe, but she wasn't Mom. It wouldn't be the same. "Maybe someday," I said. But I didn't mean it.

~ ~ ~

Sunday was the last full day of shiva. Roz stopped by in the morning before catching a plane back to L.A. She was wearing a purple pantsuit with a white fur collar and spiky purple boots. I could hardly believe it!

Before she left, she pressed a piece of paper into my hands. "This is my phone number," she said, looking directly at me. "I want you to use it. Whenever. I mean it. Don't worry about the time change or the long-distance charges. Your mother used to call constantly, so your father's used to the bills. You call me, Cara. Okay?"

"Okay," I promised.

Then she hugged me, and I could smell her shampoo, fresh and clean.

She hugged my dad goodbye, too, and whispered something to him that I couldn't hear. They both looked at me, so I knew they were talking about me. I pretended not to notice, but I hoped she'd said, Talk to Cara, David. She really needs you now.

Most of Sunday afternoon I sat with Justin. I guess my big-sister instincts took over because I felt I had to cheer him up. After all, he was only eight, and his best friend had just died. I imagined how I would feel if Marlee died. Out of habit, I pictured my thought floating up to God, but then I reeled it back in quick as I could, reminding myself that I didn't believe in that silly superstition anymore.

While we were sitting at Papa's card table, playing checkers, Justin told me, "You know, I saw the fire. That morning—I was there."

I looked up from the board and saw Justin's face, filled with fear. I hadn't thought about it, but Justin lived five houses down from us. Of course he'd seen the fire.

"The sirens woke me up," he said. "I know this sounds horrible, Cara, but I thought, Cool, a fire!" Justin said it with his eyes wide and sad, as if he couldn't believe he'd thought that.

I just nodded. Then, in a voice so quiet I barely recognized it as my own, I asked, "What did you see?"

Justin took a deep breath. "I was outside with my parents and all the other neighbors. At first, I didn't even know it was your house . . . but then I saw your dad. He was sitting on a stretcher, and he was breathing into a mask. I didn't see Janie. Or you. Or your mom. And I got really scared. My mom kept saying not to worry. But the flames were so hot, and there was thick black smoke coming out of the windows and even the roof. You wouldn't believe it."

Justin studied the checkerboard. I didn't know if he had finished talking about the fire or not.

He moved his red piece. "Your turn," he said.

My heart skipped a beat. "Wait a minute. Finish the story. What happened next?"

Justin shook his head. "Uh-uh."

"Come on, Justin. Tell." I stared hard at him, pleading with my eyes.

Justin looked around the room, then whispered, "All of a sudden my mom grabbed me and started walking me back to our house." He leaned in as if he were about to tell me a secret. I leaned in, too. Justin blinked, and tears collected in his big brown eyes. "But I saw. I saw them carry Janie out."

"Oh, Justin."

"Now I can't forget it. She was like a rag doll or something."

Justin wiped his eyes, and I blinked back my own tears.

"Justin, you have to get that picture out of your head. Just erase it and think of Janie playing soccer with you instead. Or basketball. Or anything."

"I know. I'm trying."

"Maybe I can help," I said. "Wait here." I got up and went to my scrapbook box. I found a picture of Janie running on the beach in Florida and brought it back to Justin. "*This* is Janie. She is not a rag doll. She hated dolls, and you know that. So get it out of your head, okay?"

Justin looked at the picture, and a smile crept into the corners of his mouth. "Okay," he said. He held the picture and looked at the checkerboard. "It's still your move."

~ four ~

Shiva finally ended on Monday morning, almost one week after the funeral. We all put on our coats and walked around the block. Zayde explained that it symbolized our return to society. I was glad to feel the cold wind bite at my cheeks, glad to be done with shiva, though I couldn't imagine what would come next.

The fire inspector and insurance agent had told Dad our house could be rebuilt, but it would take three to six months because of the extensive repairs needed. The first floor was badly burned, and the second floor had suffered structural damage from the heat of the fire. Mrs. Rosen had arranged for us to rent an apartment while Dad figured out what to do next.

After lunch, Dad and I got into his car and headed to the new apartment. I didn't let myself think about the car crashing the way I would have before the fire. I knew God was not listening to my thoughts and worries, protecting me. If Dad's car were to suddenly swerve on a patch of ice and hit a telephone pole or something, it would be because of the ice, the car, Dad, and the telephone pole. God was not in the picture at all. It was a strange feeling, almost like riding in the car without a seat belt.

I watched as we left the high-rises and gray slush of the city behind us. When we got closer to our neighborhood I asked, "Can we go by the house?"

"Why do you want to do that?"

I shrugged. "I don't know. I want to see it."

Dad looked at his watch and sighed. "Okay."

He slowed the car as we drove down our street. When our house came into view, I couldn't believe it. My mouth felt dry and my stomach wobbly. Yellow caution tape fenced the yard. Black smoke stains ran along the brick walls. Wooden boards covered the windows. And teddy bears, flowers, and half-deflated balloons lay in a big pile on the front lawn. I looked at my bedroom window over the garage. I imagined being stuck inside, in the dark, in the smoke. I shuddered.

I thought Dad would stop the car and we would take some of the bears and things back to the new apartment.

But he just looked out the window and shook his head. He slammed his fist on the steering wheel, the way he did sometimes when Janie and I would fight too loudly in the backseat. Then he drove away. I turned around and watched the house get smaller and smaller until it was gone.

I held back my tears. I concentrated on breathing. I looked out the window and counted the naked trees until we got to the apartment.

"So what do you think?" Dad asked, opening the door to Apartment 9, Janie's favorite number.

"It's okay, I guess." I looked around and noticed furniture in all the rooms. People had been donating all kinds of things to us since the fire, but I couldn't believe they would give us furniture. "Where did all this stuff come from anyway?"

"The apartment comes this way. It's furnished."

"So none of this belongs to us?"

"Well, no. We're renting the apartment and all the things inside of it. Look over here," Dad said, walking to the window in the living room. "See." He pointed. "There's downtown Walden. And there's your school. You won't have to take the bus anymore. You can walk or ride your bike."

"I don't have a bike anymore," I said, thinking of my red mountain bike, probably melted in our garage.

Dad looked at me. "Your bike is fine, Cara."

"It is?"

"Yes. It's in storage. When I went to the house with the fire inspector, he helped me box up and store whatever could be saved before they boarded up the house."

"Really? There's more than just my socks and underwear?"

"Yes, but not much. I'll get everything out of storage soon. But tomorrow I'm going back to work, and you're going back to school."

School? How could I do something as normal as going to school?

"Do I have to go tomorrow?"

Dad leaned against the gray wall and closed the window blinds, blocking out the bit of sunshine that had crept into the apartment. "Yes, Cara. Everyone says the sooner we get back to our normal routine, the easier it will be."

"But, Dad . . ."

He rubbed his temples. "Listen, Cara, I don't want to argue. I don't have the energy to argue. You're going back to school tomorrow, and I'm going back to work. Case closed."

He looked at me with his tired eyes, and I knew it was pointless to try to explain that I really needed to spend time with him without a million other people. That I was afraid to face everyone and everything at school. That without Mom and Janie, my routine would never be normal again.

"Fine," I mumbled, looking at the gray, worn carpet.

"I'm going to take a shower," Dad said. "Why don't you unpack your bedroom? Bubbe and Zayde are planning to stop by before they head to the airport."

From my bedroom window, I could see the building's swimming pool, covered for the winter. Would we be here in the summer? This place felt like a hotel to me. Not a home. I started to unpack my stuff. Maybe that would help. I put the two framed pictures Marlee had given me on the dresser. I put my scrapbook and supply box next to them. I put my clothes—the ones I'd worn to Marlee's, the ones I had packed for the sleepover, and my rescued socks and underwear—in the top drawer. That was it. That was all my old stuff. Everything else was either new, handed down by the Rosens, or donated by the synagogue. On the bedside table was a clock radio and a telephone. It was 3:15. Marlee was probably just getting home from school. I dialed her number.

Marlee picked up on the second ring.

"Hello?"

"Hey, Mar."

"Hey, Cara, where are you?"

"I'm at our new apartment. I don't even know our phone number. What did it come up as on your caller I.D.?"

"Same as before."

"Well, at least that's one thing that didn't change." I lay on the bed and propped my feet against the wall.

"I think my mom arranged it. Hey, have you and your dad talked at all?"

"Not about anything important. Can I come to your house after school tomorrow?"

"Sure."

I heard a click. "Oh, wait, that's call waiting. Hang on a minute. Hello?"

"Hello, is this Julia's Kitchen?" It was a lady's voice I didn't recognize.

"Um, I think you have the wrong number," I said, sitting up straight and feeling my heart race.

"I'm sure I dialed the right number."

"Yes, but this isn't Julia's Kitchen anymore." I clicked back to Marlee, my heart pounding. "Marlee?"

"Yeah?"

"That was weird."

"What?"

"Someone just called for Julia's Kitchen."

"Oh, that *is* weird. You okay?"

"I guess," I said. But my hands were shaking.

~ ~ ~

Later, Bubbe and Zayde came by with bags and bags of stuff. Tons of groceries. And things for the kitchen. Baking pans, measuring cups, even a brand-new Mixmaster. I didn't know who Bubbe bought all that stuff for, but I could tell it made her feel good to stock our kitchen as if it were a real kitchen for a real family, so I just said thank you and helped her find a place for everything.

"You're sure you're going to be okay?" Bubbe asked Dad. "We can stay longer if you want." Bubbe and Zayde had their coats on, and Zayde had been trying to leave for the last five minutes. Bubbe kept finding more things she needed to do. I knew she wasn't ready to go, and I wasn't ready to give her up.

"No," Dad said. "We'll be fine. We need to get back to normal. Right, Cara?"

I shrugged. The idea of getting back to normal seemed as crazy as Bubbe stocking our kitchen the way she would if Mom were alive.

"Come on, dear," Zayde said. "We're going to miss our plane. Cara and David have each other, and we're just a phone call away."

Bubbe hugged me tight. "You call me, love, if you need me."

My stomach felt queasy, and my water-faucet eyes turned on again. "I will," I whispered in her ear.

I hugged Zayde goodbye. "I love you, Cara," he said.

"Love you, too, Zayde."

He wiped a tear from his eye, and then they left.

Dad put his hand on my shoulder. "You okay?"

I shook my head. I wanted to be okay. I wanted to be able to get back to normal. I knew that's what Dad wanted me to do. But how?

Dad ran his hands through his hair and looked at me with his sad, sad eyes. I thought one strong wind could knock him over. I remembered the night I saw him crying. And what Zayde had just said about our having each other. I bit my lower lip. I knew I had to be strong for him. "I'll be fine," I said. "Don't worry." And I forced myself to smile.

That night I couldn't fall asleep. I heard upstairs neighbor sounds. Downstairs neighbor sounds. Next-door neighbor sounds. It drove me crazy. And then a baby cried. At least, it sounded like a baby. It cried and cried, and nobody comforted it. Every once in a while it would stop, only to start up again a few minutes later. It sounded so close, I thought it could be inside our apartment. What if someone had dropped a baby off at our front door? I told myself that was ridiculous. That didn't happen in real life. But I kept hearing the crying, and I kept wondering, so I finally got out of bed to see.

Once I left my room, I realized that the cry was coming from the hallway. I was scared to open the door. It was dark out, and late, and kind of spooky. But what if it was a baby? Shouldn't I open the door?

The crying stopped, and I stood there, deciding what

to do. I waited a full minute, counting one-Mississippi, two-Mississippi in my head.

I cracked open the door, leaving the chain lock attached. At first I saw nothing. But as I searched the hall, a cat came into view. And it wasn't just any cat.

It was Sport.

Could it be?

The cat stared at me from the shadows at the end of the hallway. A brown-and-white tabby with white paws. Just like Sport.

"Sport?" I called, my voice trembling.

If I could get closer, I'd know for sure. But behind the cat the stairwell door was propped open. If I moved too fast, the cat would run away.

Sport had a black freckle on the tip of his pink nose. Did this cat?

Quietly I unlocked the chain and stepped into the hall. "Here, Sport," I said, rubbing my hands on the hallway carpet. Sport always loved that sound.

The cat sniffed the air and took a few steps closer.

"That's right, boy, come on," I urged. I reached out, palm down, and wiggled my fingers.

The cat meowed and stepped into the pool of light.

Pink nose. No freckle.

I slumped to the floor and let out the breath I didn't know I'd been holding. It was all so unfair.

I closed my eyes and saw the real Sport. I saw our family at the animal shelter, and I saw Sport, as a kitten, climbing the walls of his cage. I saw Janie's face light up, and I heard her say, "That's the one, Daddy. Oh, please, can we get him?"

We took turns holding him. He was so small and soft and warm. He dug his tiny claws into Janie's sweater, climbed up her chest, perched himself on her shoulder, and purred in her ear.

It was hard to know if we adopted Sport or if Sport adopted Janie. But ever since that day, Sport belonged to Janie, no doubt about it.

That was it! I could adopt this cat. To remind me of Sport, and Janie, and everything normal. How perfect!

I opened my eyes, but the cat was gone. I looked up and down the hall.

Had I imagined him?

I sat in the hall for the longest time. I felt as if someone had glued me to the floor. I thought and thought about everything that had happened. Mom and Janie were dead. They weren't coming back. It was just Dad and me for-ever. At my Bat Mitzvah, at my graduations, at all my birthdays, at every special occasion and even at the not-so-special occasions, it would be just Dad and me. How would that ever be enough?

~ five ~

The next morning I convinced Dad that I could get to school on my own. It would have been too weird getting ready with Dad around instead of Mom. Dad didn't know that I liked apple juice, not orange juice. Or that I always poured my milk into a glass first before pouring it on my cereal. I didn't want to explain all these details. I just wanted him to know.

When he left for work, even though the apartment was too quiet, I felt relieved. I thought about crawling back into bed and skipping school. I was tired, and scared to face everyone at school. Mom wasn't there to make me go. I could do whatever I wanted.

So I did. I got right into bed and pulled the covers

over my head. The sheets smelled like hotel sheets. Even that was hard. As if it weren't enough that we'd lost Mom and Janie in the fire, we'd lost most of our things, too. I tried to picture everything that had been in my room: my posters, my glass animal collection, my seashell collection, all my stuffed animals, which Mom had kept asking me to donate to Goodwill, and of course my scrapbooks.

I might have stayed in bed all day if Marlee hadn't called.

"My mom's driving me to school on her way to work, so we can pick you up," Marlee said.

She tried to sound casual, but I saw right through her. Mrs. Rosen never drove Marlee to school. She took the school bus every day.

"We'll be out front at 7:55," Marlee said. "Be ready."

Marlee hung up so quickly, she didn't give me a chance to protest.

~ ~ ~

At Foster Elementary School, the kindergarten-through-third-grade wing was near the front of the building, and the fourth-through-sixth-grade classes were in the back. Marlee and I had to walk right past Janie's class to get to ours.

The hall was crowded, but people made a path for us.

Everyone stared, and some kids whispered and pointed. Marlee put her arm around my waist and guided me through the mess.

Miss Woloshin, Janie's teacher, stood in her doorway. She waved us over as we approached. Marlee and I had both had Miss Woloshin in third grade. She was one of our favorites.

"How are you, Cara?" she asked, putting her hands on my shoulders.

I shrugged, trying to be brave.

"Come in for a minute," she said.

Kids filed in and got settled at their desks. I saw Justin sitting in the front row. I waved to him, and he gave me a halfway smile. Marlee and I followed Miss Woloshin to the back of her room.

"My heart is broken, Cara," Miss Woloshin said in a quiet voice. "I can only imagine how hard this must be for you and your father. If you need anything, anything at all, you come on down to my room. Okay?"

"Okay," I said.

Miss Woloshin looked as if she were trying to make up her mind about something. Then she took a shopping bag down from a shelf and handed it to me. "I was going to call your dad to give him Janie's things, but maybe you'd like to take them. There's not much. Just her journal, her supplies, her eraser collection."

"Thanks," I said, hugging the bag to my chest. It smelled like erasers. All of a sudden I realized that's what Janie had smelled like—erasers.

The bell rang. "We better get going," Marlee said.

The rest of the day dragged. My teacher, Mr. Temby, welcomed me back but didn't make a big deal out of everything, which was fine with me. I could tell some of the kids in my class were trying hard not to stare at me.

After lunch the school social worker came into our room. Mrs. Block's name did not fit her at all. She was so skinny, she should have been named Mrs. Pencil. She usually came to get John Keeler or Colin Shapiro. They were always in trouble.

She walked over to Mr. Temby and talked quietly to him. Then Mr. Temby called my name and motioned for me to come to his desk. It was so embarrassing.

"Can I borrow you for a few minutes, Cara?" Mrs. Block asked.

I shrugged. She didn't seem to be really asking. The next thing I knew, I was following her down the hall.

Her room was tiny and windowless. I wondered if it had been a closet at one point. Posters of sunflowers covered the walls. Mrs. Block sat behind her desk, and I took the chair opposite her.

"So, Cara, this is your seventh and last year at Foster, and it's the first time we've met."

I shrugged.

"It's nice to meet you. I've heard good things about you."

I shrugged again and smiled a little. I was becoming very good at shrugging, I realized.

Mrs. Block reached over to a candy jar at the corner of her desk and slid it in front of me. "Creme Saver?"

I took a raspberry Creme Saver, unwrapped it, and popped it into my mouth.

Mrs. Block smiled. Then her face turned serious. "Cara, I am so sorry about your loss. I know this must be a terribly hard time for you and your father. And I want you to know I'm here for you if you need someone to talk to."

"Thank you," I said, nodding.

Mrs. Block looked right at me and sighed. I couldn't decide if I liked her or not. Strangely enough, the thought of talking to a complete stranger about Mom and Janie appealed to me. But where would I start?

"You know, Cara, grief is the toughest thing you'll ever encounter. Everybody deals with it at some point, but when it's happening to you, you feel so alone—as if you're the only person in the world who has ever experienced it. You might feel sad, or angry, or guilty, or anything, really. There are no wrong feelings when it comes to grief. But the best thing you can do is talk to somebody you trust about those feelings. Is there someone you would feel comfortable sharing them with?"

I thought about Dad. I wished we could talk, but I was afraid if I put the weight of my sadness on him, he'd break in two. And then there was Bubbe. I could talk to Bubbe, but would it be the same over the phone? Finally, I considered Marlee. "My best friend, Marlee Rosen," I said. "She's good at listening."

Mrs. Block smiled. "That's great, Cara. But I want you to know you can talk to me, too. Anytime. Sometimes it helps to confide in a grownup." She marked something down on her calendar. "If you don't come to see me on your own, I'll check back with you in about a week, and we'll visit then. Okay?"

I shrugged again. But this time it meant okay.

I spent the rest of the day daydreaming, watching the clock, thinking about the bag of Janie's stuff. Eventually, the final bell rang and I let out a sigh. I'd survived.

~ ~ ~

After school, I went to Marlee's. It was strange to see the usual piles of clutter stacked on the counters, the mess of shoes and backpacks by the back door, the Disney characters smiling at me from coat hooks, bookends, even kitchen tiles above the stove. It was as if nothing had changed.

Mrs. Rosen was an attorney, but she worked at her office only while Marlee and Max were in school. The rest of the time, she multitasked at home. Today she was talking on the phone, taking notes on a legal pad, and setting out a snack for us as we walked into the kitchen.

We grabbed two Cokes and some cheese and crackers and headed for Marlee's room. I hesitated in the doorway, not feeling right. The last time I had been here was the day of the fire.

"You okay?" Marlee asked, chomping on a cracker and getting crumbs all over her bed.

"I guess," I said. "It's kind of weird, though."

"Which part?"

I went in and sat on Marlee's Disney Princess beanbag chair. "All of it. I mean, everything here seems so . . . normal. I feel like a visitor from another planet."

"Which planet?"

"Huh?"

"Which planet are you from?"

"I don't know . . . Mars."

"Oh, I thought you were going to say Uranus," Marlee said, grinning.

"Marlee!" Even though we were too old for Uranus jokes, I laughed. And before long, I felt right at home again in Marlee's house.

We listened through the wall as Max practiced for his Bar Mitzvah, and we giggled every time his voice cracked. I told Marlee about the Sport look-alike, and the apartment, and how Dad still wouldn't talk about the fire.

"It's strange," I said. "I get the feeling he thinks if we don't talk about it, it'll be like it never actually happened. But not talking about the fire means not talking about Mom and Janie, too. So instead of making the fire disappear, it makes them disappear."

"Well you're just going to have to make him talk about it, that's all."

"Easy for you to say. My dad is like a ghost of himself."

"Hmmm . . ." Marlee said. She searched through a pile of papers on her desk until she found two folded pieces of newspaper. She handed them to me.

I knew what they were at once—the articles.

Suburban Blaze Kills Mother and Daughter
Father Escapes

There it was. The truth for the world to see. And there was my house in flames. I thought about Justin not recognizing our house at first, and I understood. I read on.

Fire swept through a two-story home on Cherokee Lane in north suburban Walden early Sunday, killing 42-year-old Julia Segal and her 8-year-old daughter, Jane, despite firefighter rescue attempts. David Segal, also 42, escaped with minor injuries.

Witnesses said both David and Julia Segal managed to escape the house, but Julia reentered to try to rescue Jane.

David attempted to reenter as well, but was driven back by smoke and fire. Another daughter, Cara, 11, was sleeping at a friend's house when the fire broke out.

Firefighters responded to the fire shortly after 6 a.m., at which time they located Julia and Jane in a bedroom on the second floor. Both victims were unconscious due to smoke inhalation. Paramedics tended to them on the scene, then transported all three victims to Walden Hospital. David was treated for smoke inhalation and released. Julia and Jane were both pronounced dead at 7:16 a.m., a hospital spokeswoman said.

Fire officials said the fire is under investigation, but that it appears to have started in the kitchen.

The second article was smaller, and there was no picture.

Electrical Short in Toaster Oven Blamed for Deadly Fire

The fire that ravaged a north suburban Walden home on Sunday, leaving a mother and daughter dead, appears to have started from an electrical short in a toaster oven. Fire inspector Bob Hilbert said beading on the toaster oven wire indicated a short. "This kind of short is one in a million," Hilbert said, "but it does happen. People should make a habit of unplugging any small kitchen appliances when not in use."

Services for the victims, Julia and Jane Segal, will be held at 10 a.m. Tuesday at the Goldman Memorial Funeral Home.

I read the articles twice before I said anything. I kept getting stuck on the words "pronounced dead." I thought about Nana saying I was lucky not to be an orphan. Maybe she was right. Maybe I was somehow lucky. After all, Dad had tried to go back into the house, too. I looked at Marlee, and all I could say was, "Whoa."

"I know," Marlee said. "But here's my idea. Why don't you show your dad the articles, and use them to kind of start a conversation?"

"You think that'll work?"

"It's worth a try."

"Okay," I said, "I'll try." I stuck the newspaper articles in my backpack and took out the bag of Janie's things from Miss Woloshin.

We read Janie's journal right away. Almost every page was about sports or Justin. We laughed at all her misspelled words. But then the inside of my nose tingled and my laughter turned to tears as I read "When I grow up, I will play baseball for the Cubs. I will be the picher. I will be an all star. Evryone will cheer for me!"

I looked at Marlee. She had tears in her eyes, too. Then she hiccuped. She closed the journal and handed it to me. "Let's see what else is in here," Marlee said, emptying the bag.

Janie actually had some cool erasers—every size and shape imaginable. I used to think it was dorky that she collected erasers, but now I could see the attraction. The soft, rubbery texture felt good in my hands, and I liked the smell. Marlee and I found an empty jar and decorated it with scrapbook supplies. She wrote Janie's name in fancy bubble letters, and I placed heart stickers around the top. Then I poured in the erasers. I knew Janie would have liked it.

Being with Marlee at her house melted something inside of me. It was as if I'd been clenching all my muscles since the morning of the fire, and finally I relaxed.

six

So this was my new life: on school days I waited until I heard Dad leave, then I got out of bed and into the shower. I dressed, ate a bowl of Frosted Flakes, made my lunch, then fought the cold winter wind as I walked to school. Every morning was the same. And every morning, when I heard the school noises, I was reminded of the quiet at home. I missed Mom and Janie the way January misses June. I actually wrote that down in class one day, but I crumpled it up before Mr. Temby could see it. I didn't feel comfortable letting him know my feelings. But I did talk to Mrs. Block every week. And I found I actually looked forward to our meetings. She had a nice way of listening, really listening. I knew I needed to talk to

Dad. I needed to show him the newspaper articles. And every morning I told myself I'd do it that night.

After school on Mondays and Wednesdays, I went to Hebrew school with Marlee. Mrs. Rosen drove us there, and Dad picked us up. It was strange because I wasn't even sure I believed in God anymore. Yet there I was, learning Hebrew, Torah stories, prayers—doing all the things I was supposed to do to get ready for my Bat Mitzvah in a little over a year. The one Mom and Janie wouldn't attend.

On Tuesdays and Thursdays I went to Marlee's house, and we hung out and did our homework together. Mrs. Rosen drove me home in time for me to make dinner. It was never anything fancy. Just macaroni and cheese or sloppy joes or something like that. I found out I was pretty good at following recipes on boxes or cans.

There was this little store, Snyder's Old-Time Market, right down the block from our apartment. Mrs. Rosen would drop me off there, and I would pick up whatever I needed before heading home. Mr. Snyder was a short man with almost no hair and round wire-rimmed glasses. He wore a white apron and kept a pencil behind his ear. He called me Miss Cara, and he made me feel like a character in a *Little House on the Prairie* book every time I entered his store. He set up an account for us, so I didn't have to worry about carrying money. I just signed for whatever I bought.

When I got home, there would always be messages on

the answering machine. A lady from synagogue wanting to know if she could organize people to make meals for us. Or someone from the PTO wanting the same thing. Messages from Bubbe, Nana, and Roz. And calls for Julia's Kitchen. The only calls I ever returned were Bubbe's. But even with Bubbe, I didn't have much to say. The calls would go something like this:

"Hi, Bubbe."

"Cara, love! How are you?"

"Fine."

"And your dad? How's he doing?"

"He's fine."

"School okay? Doing your homework?"

"Yep. I've got a lot."

"Well, I won't keep you. I just wanted to say I love you, and that Zayde and I are thinking of you."

"I love you, too, Bubbe. Bye."

The person I wanted to talk to—no, needed to talk to—was Dad, and I always had it in my mind that I'd show him the articles before we finished dinner.

We'd sit down to eat and Dad would ask me something about my day, and I'd answer him, but I could tell he wasn't listening. His eyes would be somewhere else. And whether I had aced a test or gotten hit in the face with a snowball, he had the same reaction: "Uh-huh." So, bite by bite, my courage would slip away. The articles would stay folded up, hidden in the spice drawer where I'd stashed them, and I'd tell myself maybe tomorrow things would be different.

Every day was pretty much the same. Except the weekends. They were worse. Instead of starting off right, with a big Shabbat dinner complete with Mom's brisket, brown potatoes, and home-baked challah, we'd order pizza. We didn't even light Shabbat candles. By Saturday afternoon, with only Ghost-Dad for company, I'd feel as if someone had scooped out my insides and left a hollow shell. So I'd escape to Marlee's. I'd sleep over on Saturday nights, and I'd tell myself not to worry about Dad, alone in the apartment.

But even at Marlee's house, things weren't normal for me. I had no desire to work on my scrapbook, despite Marlee's begging. And when we watched movies, I stopped myself from laughing too hard, even at the funniest parts. Once, I thought Marlee seemed exasperated with me, but I couldn't help it.

So January turned to February, and on February 1, Dad was watching the Super Bowl with a bag of microwave popcorn in his lap. He looked so alone, sitting on the couch without Janie. She had loved to watch sports with him. She knew every player's name and position, strengths and weaknesses. I couldn't care less about that stuff. But I sat down next to Dad anyway.

"Who's playing?" I asked.

Dad looked at me funny. "Panthers and Patriots."

"Oh." Awkward silence. "Which ones are the Panthers?"

"The ones in the white jerseys."

"Oh." Another awkward silence.

Then Dad said, "You know, Cara, you don't have to do this."

I looked at him hard.

"I know you don't like football."

I shook my head. "That's not true. I just don't really *know* football."

Dad shrugged.

I sat there until halftime. Dad was right. I didn't like football. The game was putting me to sleep. But I didn't want to admit it. And sitting there so close to Dad, even though I felt in my heart he wished I was Janie, somehow felt good to me. Maybe someday I would like football. Maybe someday Dad would love me the way he had loved Janie. The way Mom had loved me.

~ ~ ~

A week later, Dad walked into the apartment carefully balancing two huge cartons in his arms.

"What are those?" I asked as I reached for one.

"Careful, Cara!"

"I got it," I said. But it was heavier than it looked, and I dropped it to the floor with a clatter and a thud. "Oh, sorry," I said, looking quickly for Dad's reaction. I was trying so hard to do everything right, not wanting to upset him in any way.

Dad let out an angry sigh and shook his head.

"I'm sorry," I said again. "I was just trying to help. What's in there?"

"Those *were* some things from the house."

My eyes opened wide. "*Our* house?"

Dad nodded and opened the box to check the contents. "I told you I put some things in storage that first day."

I looked at the two boxes, which suddenly didn't seem so big. "That's everything?"

"These and your bike. It's in a bike room downstairs."

I couldn't believe it.

Dad pulled a framed wedding photo of him and Mom out of the box. I hadn't expected any pictures to survive the fire, and now I wondered if there were more.

"It's still in one piece," Dad said. He sat at the kitchen table and smiled a sad sort of smile. Then he looked at me. "Someday you'll look just like her." He jutted his chin to the side and stared at the picture.

My heart thumped heavily. I knew I looked like Mom. Dad used to love that about me. He'd even called me Julia Junior last Thanksgiving when I'd put on lip gloss and blush. But now, I suddenly realized, that might be the problem. Maybe my resembling Mom was why Dad never

seemed able to look me in the eyes. I was a constant reminder of what he'd lost.

I looked over Dad's shoulder at the wedding picture.
They were so young. Dad with no gray hair and a thinner
face. Mom looking at him with love in her eyes. I put my
hand gently on Dad's back. I wanted him to look at me
again. To see me, not Mom. "What else is in there?" I
whispered.

Dad shook his head as if he were waking up from a
daydream, and I pulled my hand away. He stood up, holding on to the wedding picture. "Not much. Almost nothing made it from the main floor of the house, and just
a few things were worth salvaging from upstairs. Listen,
Cara, I've decided to sell the house."

My mouth opened as if I had something to say, but
nothing came out.

"It would be a huge headache to rebuild," Dad explained, "and we don't need all that space anyhow."

"Oh," I said, and forced myself to swallow the lump
that had formed in my throat. "But where will we live?"

"Here for now. We'll see what the future holds. We
won't be homeless, Cara, I promise." Dad sighed. "I'm
tired. It's been a long day. Feel free to go through these
boxes yourself. I'm going to lie down."

What? Dad was leaving me alone with those boxes?
Those two boxes held everything that was left from our
house. Everything. It wasn't fair. None of this was fair! I

wanted to grab Dad and make him see me. His living daughter. His daughter who needed him. But I just stood there, shocked into silence.

He picked up a magazine, went to his room, and closed the door. I stared at the boxes. I noticed my breath coming faster, shallower. I knew I had to do something now!

I stomped into the kitchen, yanked open the spice drawer, and grabbed the newspaper articles. Then I marched to his room and knocked on the door. Hard.

"Come in," Dad said.

I took a breath and opened the door. "It's not fair," I said, holding up the articles.

Dad looked at me, his face blank.

I waved the articles in his face. "This is what I know about the fire. This! Two stupid newspaper articles."

Dad took the papers from me and slowly unfolded them.

"It was my house, too, Dad! My mother. My sister. And I wasn't there."

"Thank God," he said quietly, still looking at the articles.

"What?"

"I *said*, Cara, thank God you weren't there."

"No, Dad! Don't you get it? If I had been there I could make sense of this. I would know what happened."

"This *is* what happened, Cara." He turned the article

with the photograph around to show me. "It's all right here."

"Daddy, no!" Tears burned my eyes. Questions I wanted to ask flared up inside me. *Why did you leave Janie behind? How did you escape? And why did you let Mom go back in the house?* But I couldn't ask them.

Dad shook his head. "I'm sorry Cara. I don't know what you want from me. I'm trying my best. Really I am."

"Can't you at least go through the boxes with me? Please?"

Dad's face hardened. "No, Cara. I just . . . can't."

I looked at him but couldn't find even a spark of the dad I knew before. "Fine," I said. "Forget it!"

Mom would have known I didn't mean "Forget it" at all. But Dad, I think, was relieved.

I left his room and dragged the boxes into my bedroom. Since he wouldn't go through them with me, I'd do it myself, and I'd keep whatever I wanted. I stared at the boxes. I was afraid to look inside, but I also couldn't wait. Once I looked, that would be it. There would be nothing else from the house or from Mom and Janie's life, nothing. I opened one box just a bit and peeked inside. Ugh, it smelled disgusting, like burnt chemicals. I sat back and picked at my nails. Come on, I told myself, do it!

Breathing only through my mouth, I opened the box completely. Right on top was my container of seashells. I imagined Dad finding it on my nightstand. I was glad he'd thought to take it. The carved wooden bowl had darkened from smoke, and the seashells needed to be washed. But as I ran my fingers over the shells, I felt myself relax, felt my anger at Dad contract into a small corner of my heart.

Underneath the shell bowl was a bunch of file folders with labels: "Insurance," "Investments," "ADF Benefits," and more. Dad's stuff. He had kept his important documents in a green metal file cabinet that must have been fireproof. I had started to push the paperwork aside when I noticed a file labeled "Personal." It took about two seconds for me to decide to check the contents. After all, it said "Personal," not "Private: Keep Out." Inside were dozens of birthday and Father's Day cards made by Janie and me. And there were cards from Mom, too. He had saved each one. I read them and tried to figure out how the dad we'd loved so much could be the same dad I knew now. It didn't make sense.

I returned the cards and tucked the "Personal" file in with the others. Then I pulled out Mom's jewelry box. The silver box was tarnished black, but inside were a bunch of Mom's earrings, necklaces, and bracelets. I picked up a gold chain with a small ruby heart pendant, and felt myself smile. Dad had given it to Mom for her birthday last year. I turned the ruby heart back and forth to catch the light. It sparkled. I put it on and looked in the mirror. It was too fancy to wear every day, but I would wear it someday—I knew it. I took the necklace off and placed it carefully back in the jewelry box.

Then I saw photographs! A whole bunch of the framed photos that had stood on Mom's dresser. Our family before the fire. A regular family. Most of the frames were stained black from smoke. The glass had melted a bit and the photos were faded, but they looked great to me. I took the photos out of the frames and studied each precious picture, memorizing the composition, the light, the expressions on our faces.

The second box held even more treasures. Janie's baseball cards. Not all of them, but I couldn't believe even one had survived. They must have been the cards she'd thrown in her desk drawer—the ones she hadn't yet stored in her plastic, meltable three-ring binder. It seemed impossible that I was holding something that had been so important to Janie.

And there were four mezuzot in the box, too. The biggest one was copper and bronze decorated with a swirly Hebrew letter *shin*. It had been screwed into the doorpost at the front entrance to our house. I rubbed the ash-stained metal with my thumb and saw that it would shine with a little cleaning. Two small silver mezuzot had been affixed to Janie's and my doorposts. And the ceramic mosaic one had graced the doorway to Mom and Dad's room. Tucked inside each of the mezuzot was the prayer scroll with the Shema printed on it. I unrolled one of the scrolls and ran my fingers over the Hebrew letters. I knew what they said. "Hear, O Israel. The Lord is our God. The Lord is One."

Shivers ran up and down my spine. How had *those* survived? Was it a message from God? How else could the mezuzot and prayers have stayed in one piece? But what was the message? Maybe God wanted me to know he did exist, only not the way I'd imagined before. Maybe God couldn't stop my house from burning down, and he couldn't protect me from a car crash or any other danger, but he was still there—doing . . . something. But what?

I rolled up the prayer scrolls and tucked them back inside the mezuzot. I didn't know what to think. But the possibility of God existing, even if I didn't understand him, comforted me. Maybe I'd hang the mezuzot in this apartment. Maybe Dad would help. After all, he'd taken them from our home. He must have wanted them if he'd gone to the trouble of unscrewing them from the doorposts.

Just when I thought I couldn't be shocked by anything else, I spotted something at the very bottom of the carton. I reached for it and gasped. Mom's black metal recipe box! I opened it and looked inside. All of Mom's recipes, in her curvy handwriting, in perfect order. Impossible! My hands shook as I held the black box.

I found my favorite recipe, chocolate-chip cookies,

and read it. I had baked them with Mom about a million times.

I considered surprising Dad tomorrow when he got home from work with a warm, chewy cookie. He would smell the apartment from the hallway. He would think he was dreaming. He would walk in and see the cookies, Mom's cookies, and . . . and . . . I didn't know what would happen next. Would it make him happy? Or would it break his heart? Hadn't he seemed so sad when he said I would look like Mom when I grew up? Besides, hadn't I sworn I would never eat another dessert?

It was a bad idea. I could never make her cookies. Who did I think I was, anyway?

~ ~ ~

On Monday after Hebrew school, Dad and I ate spaghetti for dinner. Then Dad turned on the TV and I went to my room and tried on Mom's ruby necklace again. I gathered all the photographs, along with Janie's journal and baseball cards and Mom's recipes. I got to work putting the photos in my scrapbook. In big block letters I printed AFTER THE FIRE across the top of a double page spread. I wished I could ask Marlee to write it, but she was definitely getting tired of my mourning. I hadn't even told her about the boxes—although I'd really wanted to.

Next I matted the pictures of Mom and Janie. I mounted a photo of Janie in the center of one page and one of Mom in the center of the other. Around their pictures, I listed some of the things I wanted to always remember about them.

On Janie's side, I wrote: Crooked Teeth, Great Athlete, Tomboy, Best Friends with Justin Wittenberg, Scared of Thunderstorms, Cat-Lover, Wanted to Pitch for the Cubs, Messy, Sweet, Sometimes Annoying.

On Mom's side, I wrote: Smelled Like Vanilla, Curly Hair, Hazel Eyes, Best Baker in the World, Helpful, Organized, Loving, Cool Mom, Sometimes Strict.

Then, across the bottom, I wrote: Died Way Too Soon.

To the next pages I attached all the rest of the photos, the baseball cards, and my favorite recipes. I even ripped out some pages of Janie's journal to put in there. I thought about what it would be like to look at this scrapbook next year, or sometime far in the future. I wondered if I would ever forget Mom and Janie. Would they someday be just these pictures and items to me? Would I forget Mom's smell or the feel of her skin? Would Janie's giggles fade away forever?

By the time I'd finished everything, it was eleven-thirty. Dad must have gone to bed without saying good night to me, or maybe he'd fallen asleep on the couch. I knew I'd be exhausted tomorrow. But if I skipped my shower in the morning and got my backpack organized now, I'd be able to sleep a little later. So I checked my assignment notebook and my folder to make sure I had everything I needed. My folder was stuffed with old papers from school. Mom used to look at all the notes and graded papers, but now they just sat in the folder.

I grabbed the papers and walked to the wastebasket. It wasn't as if Dad would care about them. But one piece of pink paper caught my eye. It was a flyer about the Valentine's Day Bake Sale. It would be this Friday, and everyone was invited to bring in baked goods. I thought about Mom's cookies from last year's sale. Janie and I had been so excited when everyone wanted to know who had made the giant, delicious, heart-shaped cookies.

That very night, we talked Mom into starting Julia's Kitchen. We sat around the dinner table, all four of us, coming up with names for the business. "That's the Way the Cookie Crumbles" was Dad's suggestion. We cracked up over that one. We thought of "Cookies and More," "Cookies Galore," "Segal's Sweets," and "Just Desserts." Then I came up with "Julia's Kitchen." Mom said she liked it because it sounded "sophisticated, sweet, and homey."

I had pictured Mom as the next Mrs. Field or Famous Amos. Not dead within a year. I crumpled the flyer and tossed it into the trash with the rest of my papers. Taking off Mom's necklace, I stared at the picture of her on the raft in Florida, and went to sleep.

~ seven ~

The day before our Valentine's Day celebration at school, Marlee and I signed valentines for the class party at her kitchen table. Personally, I thought we were too old to pass out those silly valentines, but Mr. Temby said that signing valentines was our homework assignment that night. The cards I'd bought at Snyder's weren't too cutesy. No little teddy bears or ducks or anything. And no hearts or lovey-dovey things either. They were just plain cards with a tie-dyed design that said, Happy Valentine's Day, Friend! Marlee's valentines were the kind you stick a lollipop through.

While we worked, the stuffed pasta shells Mrs. Rosen was making for dinner bubbled and baked in the oven, and we breathed in the smells of garlic and melted mozzarella. I was halfway through the class list, going alphabetically. Marlee didn't look at the list. She just wrote out the cards as she thought of the kids in our class.

Max came into the kitchen and swiped a lollipop off the table.

"Hey, give it!" Marlee said.

Max ripped open the plastic and shoved the lollipop into his mouth. "Oops! Too late," he said, grinning. "Unless you want it now." He held the wet candy in front of Marlee's face.

"You're disgusting," she said.

I tried not to smile. Max was funny even if he was annoying. He pulled out a chair, turned it around, and sat on it backwards. "So, you're getting all ready for the annual Foster Valentine's party? I remember it like it was yesterday."

"Duh, Max. You're just one year ahead of us," Marlee said. She rolled her eyes at me.

"Yeah, but junior high is another world. You'll see."

"Whatever." Marlee stuck another lollipop through a valentine. "Don't you have any homework, Mr. Cool Junior High Student? Or maybe you should practice for your Bar Mitzvah. Just be sure you put any glass away before you start singing."

Max ignored Marlee's last comment. "I'm taking a break," he said. "I wanted to know what you guys are baking for the bake sale. Wondering when there will be a spoon to lick."

Marlee looked at me. I stared at my valentines and picked my nails. Marlee and I had already discussed the bake sale. I'd told her I wasn't baking, and she had seemed to understand. But now I thought maybe she wanted to bake and felt I wasn't letting her.

"What?" Max asked. "They still have the bake sale, don't they?"

"Yes," Marlee said, glaring at Max. "They still have the bake sale."

"So what are you making?"

"I don't know!" Marlee shouted.

I noticed she hadn't said, Nothing.

"Jeez. Calm down," Max said, getting up from the table. "I was just asking."

Max left the room and whispered under his breath, "Brownies are always a good choice."

Marlee blew her bangs out of her eyes. "We don't have to bake anything," she said to me.

"But you want to," I said.

Marlee grinned, caught. "Well, it is fun to bake brownies. And we haven't done anything really fun since . . . well, you know."

No, I thought. It would not be fun. It would be sad and empty and unfair to Mom.

"I wouldn't make you do it, Cara. I mean, it's totally

up to you. I know you said you didn't want to bake, and I get it, but . . . Mr. Temby did promise extra credit to kids who brought in baked goods, and I sure could use some of that." Marlee raised her eyebrows and tilted her head to the side. "So?"

I was torn between wanting to satisfy Marlee and needing to be loyal to Mom. "Can't you just bake tonight, after I leave?"

Marlee sighed. "I guess. But, Cara, come on. It'd be more fun if we did it together. We've never done that. And who knows? It might actually make you happy."

I doubted that. But Marlee was my best friend. I supposed I could do this for her. "Oh, fine, fine, fine! Let's do it." I tossed my pen aside and stacked my valentines in a pile.

"Really?"

"Really. Before I change my mind."

Marlee's grin spread across her face. "All right . . . if you insist." She got up and pulled out a box of Duncan Hines brownie mix from the pantry. "Brownies it is!"

I took a deep breath and set about finding a bowl and spoon.

"We need two eggs, water, and oil," Marlee said, reading the box.

We never used mixes at our house. And we never baked with oil. Pure, unsalted butter, Mom used to say. No substitutions.

Marlee ripped open the plastic and poured the brownie mix into the Disney Villains bowl I'd found. She poured it in too fast, sending a chocolate dust cloud into her face, which made her sneeze. I measured the oil, then the water, carefully looking at the measuring cup from the side. Marlee cracked the eggs.

"Oops, I think I got some shell in there," she said, peering into the bowl. She started to put her finger in the bowl to fish the eggshell out.

"Wait. Let me see," I said. I took one of the eggshells and used it as a spoon to remove the other shell. The shells acted like magnets and stuck to each other easily.

"Cool," Marlee said.

"Trick of the trade," I said. I felt that I'd always known the eggshell trick. Mom must have taught me. I'd never baked anything without her before today. Was she watching me now? If she was, what was she feeling? Was she happy? Sad? Proud? Were her feelings as mixed up as mine?

We had to stir fifty strokes by hand, so we took turns, twenty-five each. I liked watching the yellow egg disappear into the brown batter as we stirred.

"I'll grease the pan," I said. I opened the refrigerator, which was covered with Disney magnets, and looked for the butter. Mom always kept a stick wrapped in wax paper just for greasing pans, but all I could find in Marlee's refrigerator was a tub of margarine. So I took a paper towel, scooped out some margarine, and spread it evenly around the pan.

"Now for my favorite part," Marlee said, pouring the batter into the pan. She scraped the sides of the bowl with the wooden mixing spoon. I knew a rubber spatula would work better, but I didn't say so. Besides, I wasn't sure the Rosens had a rubber spatula.

Marlee smoothed out the batter, then popped the spoon into her mouth. "Mmm . . ." she said, licking her lips. "You want the bowl?"

I shook my head. I had loved licking the bowl clean when Mom and I baked, but this was different. This didn't feel like real baking to me. It felt like a shortcut. An imitation. Besides, I reminded myself, I had sworn off desserts forever—baked or raw.

"You take it," I said. "Or let's leave it for Max."

"Max who?" Marlee said, digging right in. She had chocolate smeared on her cheeks and chin.

I opened the oven and slid the brownie pan onto the shelf below the stuffed shells. But as I pulled my hand out, I accidentally brushed the top oven rack.

"Ow!" I yelled, yanking my hand back. The skin looked pink where it burned. I turned on the cold water and shoved my hand under the faucet.

"Are you okay?" Marlee asked.

My heart raced. The cold water numbed my skin and took away the pain. "I guess," I said.

Marlee put her arm around me. "You're shaking," she said.

Just then the White Rabbit popped out of his clock and said, "Six o'clock! I'm late! I'm late!"

I started to cry. I couldn't help myself. I felt like such a baby.

"It's okay," Marlee said. "Mom!" she called.

Mrs. Rosen ran into the kitchen. "What's wrong?" she asked. "What happened?"

"Cara burned herself on the oven."

"Oh dear, let me see," Mrs. Rosen said. She took my hand and turned it side to side. It already had started to blister.

I tried to catch my breath.

"There, now. You're going to be okay, Cara. Just keep it under the faucet."

After my hand was frozen numb, I sat at the kitchen table while Mrs. Rosen squeezed Neosporin onto the burn and covered it with a Band-Aid. I thought about Mom and Janie. In the house. In the fire.

"I knew I shouldn't have baked," I said. Marlee looked hurt, but I didn't care. "I want to go home."

Mrs. Rosen nodded. She looked close to tears, too. "Of course, honey. Let me get my coat."

"No," I said suddenly. "I'll call my dad." I didn't know why, but I wanted my dad.

~ ~ ~

In the car on the way home, Dad listened to his sports radio station. I leaned my head against the window and looked out, but all I could see was my own reflection staring back at me. What had happened the night of the fire? How had Dad gotten out without Mom and Janie? The pain in my hand returned, throbbing.

I felt the vibration of every crack in the street as our tires rolled over them, tha-thunk, tha-thunk, tha-thunk. And then I heard a voice. A small voice, like Janie's. It said, Ask him, ask him, ask him.

I sat up straight and looked at Dad. He hadn't heard a thing. Had I imagined the voice, like the Sport look-alike? I leaned back against the window and listened hard. Ask him, ask him, I heard.

No, I thought. I had tried that. It was too soon. Dad wasn't ready. Unless, maybe . . . maybe I'd gone about it in the wrong way. I'd been angry because of the boxes. I'd shoved the articles in his face. Not a very warm invitation to a conversation. Maybe I could be calm, talk to him nice and easy, the way Mrs. Block talked to me.

I felt butterflies in my stomach. But they weren't butterflies. They were words. Words that bubbled up and finally spilled out of my mouth. "Dad, can we talk about the fire?" I asked quietly.

Dad glanced at me, then went back to watching the road.

I reached over and turned off the radio, surprising myself with my courage. "I need to know what happened."

Dad sighed and looked straight ahead. "You know what happened, Cara," he said wearily.

"No, I don't. Not really."

"The fire started from the toaster oven."

"Well, I know that, but what *happened*? How did you get out of the house without them?"

Dad shook his head and didn't say anything for a minute. Then, "Cara, I can't . . . I—I don't want to . . . I'm trying my best to forget that night and to remember everything from before. That's what you should do, too. Just be glad you weren't there."

I felt as though he had punched me in the stomach. How could I forget about the fire when it was such a mystery to me? I always figured that at some point Dad and I would talk about it, and I would finally understand what had happened. A whole month had gone by. I thought that must be enough. But now I knew he would never talk about the fire.

Stinging tears filled my eyes. If Dad had died in the fire instead of Mom, everything would have been different. Mom would have talked to me. She would have explained it all. She wouldn't have made me feel like an orphan. She would have made everything okay.

I turned away from Dad and stared back at my reflection in the window. I didn't want to see myself, so I closed my eyes.

"Cara?" Dad asked. "Do you understand?"

I didn't answer him. I didn't want to ever talk to him again.

~ ~ ~

The next day at school Mr. Temby announced, "Okay, everybody, time to pass out your valentines."

My valentines! I'd left them at Marlee's. Ugh! Would nothing ever go right for me? There was a great rumble of activity as everyone dug their valentines out from their desks. I walked over to Marlee.

"I think I left my valentines at your house, Mar. Did you bring them?"

"Oh, really? That stinks! I didn't see them."

"But they were right next to yours."

"I don't think so. I would have noticed." Marlee pulled her valentines out of a Ziploc bag.

I stood there picturing my stack of cards hidden under some pile at the Rosens'. "Well, what am I supposed to do?" I asked.

"How should I know?"

"Marlee!"

"What?"

But I didn't get to respond because Marlee was on her feet, passing out her valentines, not worried at all about me.

I sulked at my desk and watched as everyone gave out their stupid cards. Why was Marlee being that way? Was she too excited about Valentine's Day to care about me? It made me mad to think about it. And jealous. Marlee's family and her house were intact. She could get excited about Valentine's Day and bake sales.

I remembered other Valentine's Days. Every year Dad would buy those heart-shaped boxes filled with chocolates for Mom, Janie, and me. He'd say that we were the loves of his life. I was pretty sure he would ignore Valentine's Day this year. And I didn't want chocolate from him anyway.

Mrs. Block poked her head into our room just then and asked to "borrow" me. So while everyone else read their valentines and ate sweets from the bake sale, I sat in the sunflower room with Mrs. Block and filled her in on the latest with Dad.

"I don't think Dad will ever explain what happened in the fire," I said.

Mrs. Block nodded. "He might not. It sounds as if he can't."

"But why not?"

"I don't know. Why do *you* think he can't?"

I picked at my nails and thought about Dad. Why couldn't he talk about the fire? Because it hurt too much? Because he felt guilty? I hadn't thought about his reasons before. I hadn't cared. I'd only cared about what I needed—a parent to take care of me. And really, didn't I deserve that?

Mrs. Block looked at me, waiting patiently for my answer.

"It doesn't matter, does it?" I asked. "His reasons, I mean. Because no matter what, it just stinks. I need him to talk about the fire, and he needs to forget about it. So there we are."

Mrs. Block nodded sympathetically. "Yes, there we are."

That night Dad and I ordered pizza and ate in front of the TV in the living room. I was sure he didn't know that tomorrow was Valentine's Day. And I wasn't about to tell him.

~ eight ~

On the way to Hebrew school the next Wednesday, Mrs. Rosen asked me if Dad and I would come for Shabbat dinner on Friday. Dad and I hadn't done anything Jewish since shiva, and even though I was confused about God, especially since I'd found those mezuzot, I knew I missed Shabbat. I missed the food, the songs, the whole tradition.

"I'm making a brisket," Mrs. Rosen added.

My mouth watered. "Thanks! I'll check with Dad after Hebrew school," I said, even though I knew it would be fine. It wasn't as if we had any other plans.

But when I told Dad about the invitation as he drove me home, he frowned and said, "I'm not up for social engagements yet, Cara."

He must have read the disappointment on my face, because then he said, "Why don't you go without me?"

I felt as if there were the thinnest thread holding Dad and me together. And if I went to the Rosens without him for Shabbat, that thread might break. But then again, if Dad didn't care, why should I?

So I went home with Marlee straight from school on Friday. Already her house felt like Shabbat. I smelled brisket, sweet potatoes, and something cinnamony. Marlee and I set the dining room table with a white lace tablecloth and Mrs. Rosen's china. No Disney plates for Shabbat. On top of each plate we placed a silver kiddush cup and filled Max's, Marlee's, and mine with grape juice and Mr. and Mrs. Rosen's with wine. Two white Shabbat candles in silver candlesticks stood in the middle of the table next to two loaves of challah.

Marlee covered the challot with an embroidered challah cover. "Perfect," she declared, admiring the table.

The table did look beautiful. But it was far from perfect. For one thing, the challah was not homemade. Plus, there were eight chairs but only five places set. If Dad had come, there would have been six, a nice even number. And Mom and Janie would have made eight—no empty spaces. But I couldn't expect Marlee to notice any of that.

"What?" Marlee said, squinting at me. "What's wrong?"

"Nothing."

"Then why are you making that face?"

"What face?"

"*That* face. Like you're about to cry."

"Oh." I hadn't realized my feelings were so obvious. "It's just . . . you know, I miss my family."

Marlee let out a big, tired sigh. "Oh."

I felt my stomach tighten. Marlee's Oh sounded like Oh no, not again.

"Am I boring you?" I joked.

But Marlee didn't smile. "No," she said. "It's just hard to hear about it all the time, that's all."

My mouth dropped open, but I shut it quickly, suddenly aware of everything my face was doing. If Marlee thought it was so hard to hear about it, she should try living it.

She blew her bangs out of her eyes. "I mean, really, Cara, I'm saying this as your best friend. Your mom wouldn't want you to sulk around forever."

"I don't sulk around. And it hasn't been forever. It's been forty-one days."

"See? You're counting the days. How can you live if you're counting the days?"

I couldn't believe I had to defend myself to Marlee. As if the time limit for my grief was up. Some friend!

"All I'm saying is, I miss the old Cara."

Didn't she know I missed the old me, too? But it wasn't as if I could snap my fingers and return to normal.

I wanted to go home, to crawl into bed and never get out. "Maybe I should go," I said, "considering I'm such a downer and all."

"No, Cara. Don't go." She touched my arm. "I didn't mean to hurt your feelings."

"Well, you did!"

"Look, I'm sorry. Let's just forget it." Marlee walked past me toward the family room.

I followed behind. "Easy for you to say! Easy for my dad to say. Everyone always wants to forget whatever's hard to talk about."

Marlee spun around to face me. I could hear Max playing GameCube in the family room. "Cara," Marlee said, "I am not like your dad! I've been here for you every day. Every minute of every day."

"And what? You've had enough?"

Marlee crossed her arms. "I don't know. Maybe I have. Look, maybe we just need a little break from each other. I mean, you come over practically every day. Maybe if we saw each other less often, I could be a better friend to you. And think about it—you could spend more time with your dad and maybe work things out."

I controlled my face as best I could. I would not let her see how much she had hurt me. I took a slow, steadying breath. "You know, you're absolutely right," I said. "I was getting tired of coming here anyhow."

Marlee glared at me, and I glared back.

So I stayed, but it was weird. Marlee and I played GameCube with Max, and both of us talked to Max but not to each other. I found myself asking God, *Why are you taking another person I love away from me?* Then I changed my mind and sent a different thought to him: *God, I am overflowing with sadness!*

Just before sundown, Mrs. Rosen and Marlee sang the prayer for lighting the Shabbat candles. I tried to sing along, but my voice wouldn't cooperate. My throat felt all closed up, as if I were about to cry. I pictured Mom, Janie, and me lighting the candles on Shabbat, and my heart felt heavy.

The flames on the candles grew, and Mrs. Rosen put her arms around me. "Shabbat Shalom," she said.

"Shabbat Shalom," I replied in a whisper.

Max led the kiddush, and his voice didn't break the whole time. Then Mr. Rosen said the motzi, the blessing over the challot, and it was time to eat.

The brisket didn't taste half as good as Mom's, and I couldn't even compare the challah. The conversation centered on Max's upcoming Bar Mitzvah. I ate quietly, keeping my eyes down.

After dinner, Dad picked me up. I went home, buried my head in my pillow, and cried.

~ ~ ~

I woke up in the morning sure that Marlee would call and apologize. She had just been cranky last night, I figured. She hadn't meant half of what she'd said. But she didn't call. And the next day at Sunday school, she pretended that nothing had happened, which might have been okay if things were normal between us. But they weren't. Not even close. When we had to pick partners for a vocabulary game, Marlee picked Shayna Mages, not me. I was so mad I didn't even say goodbye to her when we dropped her off at her house.

That afternoon Dad went to work. He'd started working even on the weekends, which made it easier for us to avoid each other. I was hungry, but all I could find in the kitchen was leftover pizza and three-day-old Chinese takeout. So I walked to Snyder's to get some bread and peanut butter. At the checkout counter, I saw thick double-sided tape. The picture on the package showed someone attaching a piece of art to a door, and it made me think of the mezuzot. They were still sitting on my dresser. We were supposed to screw the mezuzot into the doorposts, but I didn't have a drill or a screwdriver or anything like that. The double-sided tape would work perfectly, so I bought it.

After eating two peanut butter sandwiches, I hung the copper and bronze mezuzah with the swirly *shin* on our front doorpost. One silver mezuzah went on the door to my bedroom. And the ceramic mosaic one that used to

hang on Mom and Dad's door—I laid it on Dad's dresser.
I figured he could put it up if he wanted. I knew I was
supposed to say a prayer when I hung the mezuzot, but I
didn't know what it was. So I made up my own.

Dear God, I thought, *I'm hanging these mezuzot because I
want to. Because I like the tradition of it. I don't know why they
were saved and Mom and Janie weren't. I used to think you ran
the world like a great big puppet show, but I don't think that
anymore. Maybe you had nothing to do with saving these mezuzot from the fire. Maybe you had nothing to do with Mom and
Janie dying. And nothing to do with Marlee being so mean.
Maybe sometimes things just happen, and you feel as bad about
them as we do.*

*After the fire, I tried not believing in you. But that didn't feel
right. Because if you don't exist, where are Mom and Janie now?
I hope they are with you, and I hope they understand what you
do. Because I sure don't. I mean, I get that you're not a big puppet master, controlling everything, but are you even out there?
Listening? Watching? Just what do you do all day? I hope you
don't mind these questions. It's just, well, that's what's on my
mind. Amen.*

I let out a big sigh.

I didn't think Dad would notice the mezuzot. But I
had the feeling Mom knew. And she was glad.

~ ~ ~

On Monday, Marlee still didn't apologize to me. Not on Tuesday either. We were nice to each other at school, in a polite kind of way, but we weren't friends. At recess, I went to the library instead of dealing with the question of whom to hang out with.

As I walked home by myself Tuesday afternoon, I thought about what Marlee had said to me. It was true that I'd been counting the days since the fire. And maybe I had been sulking. But jeez, my house had burned down! My mom and sister had died, and my dad was barely talking to me. What did she expect? She said she missed the old Cara. The way I missed the old Dad. If only I knew how to get us both back.

I went into the empty apartment and pressed PLAY on the answering machine.

The first message was from Nana. "Hello, David. This is your mother." As if he didn't know her voice. "I've tried calling you at work, but you haven't returned my calls. Maybe your secretary isn't giving you the messages." So, I wasn't the only one who liked to avoid Nana. "Please call me. Oh, and give my love to Cara."

I pressed ERASE and wrote "Dad, call Nana," on a piece of paper, even though I doubted he'd call her.

The next message was from Bubbe. "Hi, David. Hi, Cara. Haven't heard from you in a while. Call me soon. Love you, love you!"

The third message was a voice I didn't recognize. "Hi. I hope this is Julia's Kitchen. My name is Renee Price."

As she started to leave her phone number, I almost hit ERASE. I was still getting calls for Julia's Kitchen, and it always made me sad that Mom couldn't take their orders. But this voice was gentle and reminded me a little of Bubbe, so I listened.

"I got your number from my friend Sheryl, who swears by your cookies. Well, my daughter just had a baby. A beautiful baby girl. And I'd like to order one of your gift baskets for her. I understand you decorate cookies with names, and I'd like a couple of those in the basket along with an assortment of your other famous cookies. Please call me to let me know if you can help. Thank you. Oh, yes, the baby's name is Julia."

I fell into the kitchen chair. Julia? My arms broke out in goose bumps. People didn't name their babies Julia anymore. They were all Emmas or Hannahs or Sarahs. Right away I picked up the phone to call Marlee. She had to hear about this. But then I remembered—we were taking a break from each other. I held the phone in my hand. A thought started to form. I could call Renee. I could take her order. I could bake the cookies and deliver them just the way Mom would have. Yes! It felt exactly right. I dialed before I could change my mind. After the second ring, someone picked up.

"Hello?" It was the same gentle voice. Renee's.

"Hi. This is Julia Segal," I lied. I lowered my voice to seem as grownup as I could without sounding phony. "I'm returning your call about the gift basket."

"Oh, hello. I'm glad you called back," said Renee. "As I said in my message, my friend Sheryl Pearlman just raved about your cookies last year. You did a darling basket for her first grandchild. And now I've joined the grand-mother club myself! I was so glad I held on to your num-ber."

"Thank you," I said. I wondered if I should pretend to remember Sheryl Pearlman, but I figured that might get me into even more trouble, so I just said, "Are you inter-ested in a small, medium, or large basket?"

"Oh, I don't know. How many cookies come in each?"

I paced the kitchen floor. I wasn't sure how many cookies came in each. I just remembered that Mom had three different sizes. "I'm sorry . . . What did you say?"

"How many cookies come in each basket?"

"Oh . . . yes . . . there are . . . a dozen cookies in a small, two dozen in a medium, and three dozen in a large." That sounded about right.

"I see. Well, then, I'll take a medium. And that will in-clude some cookies with Julia's name on them, right?"

"Yes. Absolutely." What was I saying? I didn't know how to decorate cookies like that.

"How much will it be?"

Stumped again. I almost hung up at that point. But instead I said, "I'm sorry. That's my other line. Can you hang on a minute?" I pressed the HOLD button and tried to regulate my breathing. Think . . . think . . . What did Mom charge for the baskets? I remembered that she'd had a color brochure printed on glossy paper. It had pictures of the baskets and treats, and I knew it had a price list. I just couldn't picture the numbers in my head. So I calculated quickly from what I knew the prices were at Snyder's. I'd have to buy chocolate chips, flour, sugar, oatmeal, raisins, eggs, and butter, not to mention the basket. Hmm . . . would $25 be enough? Did that sound right? I took a deep breath and clicked back to Renee.

"Hi. So sorry about that. It will be $25."

"Is that all? Well, at that price, I might as well go for a large." Renee laughed, and I cringed.

"Okay. The large is . . . $35." And then, thinking quickly, I said, "Cash only. And you can pay my delivery girl."

She told me she wanted the basket next Monday, March 1, and I felt another round of goose bumps. That was Mom's birthday. I scribbled down the address where the basket was to go: 1414 Baer Avenue in Longridge. Longridge! How would I get there? At least school would be closed that day and I'd have plenty of time.

I hung up the phone and thought about what I'd just

done. Was I crazy? How was I supposed to bake three dozen of my mother's best cookies, including those special "name" cookies, prepare the gift basket, and get it to Renee's daughter's house by March 1? And what if Dad found out what I was doing? Impersonating my mother. Lying to a stranger. I was pretty sure he would *not* understand.

Still, I couldn't deny that energy was buzzing through my body. I felt alive. I felt like jumping up and down.

I hurried into my room, took out my scrapbook, and turned to Mom's recipes. Chocolate-chip cookies, oatmeal raisin, peanut butter, snickerdoodle, the choices went on and on. Where would I ever begin? It was funny that so many of the cookies had the same ingredients, more or less. Snickerdoodles were actually chocolate-chip cookies, minus the chocolate chips, plus some cinnamon sugar. And cinnamon sour cream twists were snickerdoodles plus yeast and sour cream.

I sorted through the recipes and finally settled on four I would attempt. Chocolate-chip cookies because they were the first ones I'd ever made with Mom. Snickerdoodles because I always liked that word. And oatmeal raisin for a change of taste. And then, of course, the name cookies, which I realized now were tea cookies with buttercream frosting. I dreaded writing the name Julia on the cookies. How could I write Mom's name on them? It would be so weird. Besides, I wasn't any good at that kind of thing. I had tried to use Mom's decorating tools a few times before, but everything I'd done had come out blotchy and uneven. If only I could ask Marlee to do it.

I was so lost in the recipes that I nearly jumped out of my skin when I heard Dad's key turn in the lock. I slammed the scrapbook shut and opened the nearest book I could find, my social studies textbook. Yuck. I tried to act natural, lying on my bed, flipping through the pages. Dad knocked on my door while opening it. I pretended to be engrossed in social studies and didn't look up.

"Hey, Cara, I'm home."

"Oh, hi," I said, giving him a quick glance before looking back at my book.

He stood there a minute, not saying a thing. "I thought you'd be at Marlee's," he finally said.

"Not today."

"I was going to order pizza. Does that sound good?"

"Fine," I said, shrugging. He stood in the doorway waiting for something. I kept reading the same line over and over. I just wanted him to leave so I could make my shopping list.

"I've got a lot of work to do," I said, looking him in the eye.

As soon as I did that, he looked at the floor. "Yeah, me too." He motioned to his briefcase. "New campaign for Kellogg's."

I turned back to my book, and he closed my door.

Would we always be like strangers with each other? I tried to remember a time when Dad was his old self, the fun dad other kids thought was so cool. I had to admit, *I* used to think he was cool. He was always smiling and joking around. I remembered the day before the fire. Dad had teased me about spending all my Saturday nights with Marlee, eating pizza and working on our scrapbooks. He'd said, "You gotta live a little, Cara." Then he'd danced me around the living room, doing some crazy version of the tango. It hadn't even bothered me when Janie cut in, begging, "My turn, Daddy! Dance with me!"

Even though he'd been closer to Janie than to me, it hadn't mattered because I'd had Mom. Now Dad was a totally different person. He wasn't even handsome anymore. He needed a haircut. His face drooped. And he always had a faraway look in his eyes.

Had my appearance changed, too? I looked in the mirror and studied my eyes. Still light brown. But when I looked closer I noticed the thinnest ring of greenish-yellow around the outside edges. Mom had said that when she was sixteen, her eyes changed to hazel. Maybe mine were on their way.

What about the rest of me? I couldn't possibly be as gloomy as my dad, as boring. Could I? Could Marlee be right about me?

~ nine ~

All day Wednesday and Thursday, instead of thinking about the fire or my fight with Marlee, I thought about baking. I liked knowing I had this big exciting secret that not even Marlee knew about.

On Thursday Mr. Temby ran out of library passes, so I had to go outside for recess. I took an extra long time putting on my jacket, hat, and gloves. I wanted to be the last one out so I could scan the playground and choose the right group to join. I spotted Marlee at the four-square court with some other kids from our class. The fifth-grade girls were playing tetherball, and the boys were making a snow fort on the field. A bunch of younger girls were having some kind of talent show by the jungle gym.

And some boys were playing basketball. That's where Janie would be if she were here—playing basketball with the boys. I saw Justin grab a rebound, and I headed over to watch.

Most of the boys had unzipped their coats and clearly would have taken them off altogether if the recess monitors weren't watching. But I was freezing just standing there. I tucked my chin and mouth inside my jacket and felt my breath warm me.

Someone made a basket, and Justin took the ball out of bounds right near me. "Hey, Cara!" he said. "Wanna play?"

I shook my head. "No thanks. Too cold."

"Oh, come on! It'll warm you up."

But I shook my head again. Playing basketball was Janie's thing. "I'll cheer you on."

"Works for me." Justin twirled the basketball on his finger. "I gotta get used to cheerleaders anyhow for when I'm in the NBA!"

"Come on, Justin," another boy shouted. "Let's go."

Justin threw the ball in, and I watched as he called all the shots, hogged the ball, and scored most of the baskets. He seemed so fine, as if his life had returned to normal, his life without Janie. I was happy for him, but I was also mad. Shouldn't he be miserable without her? Marlee wouldn't think so. She'd probably wish I'd take a lesson from Justin.

When the bell rang to end recess, Justin asked me if I would come to his basketball game on Saturday night. His team was playing in the championship.

I wanted to say no, but the thought of spending Saturday night at home with Dad was enough to make me forgive Justin for being happy. "Okay," I said. "I'll be there."

As soon as school let out, I headed to Snyder's.

"Hello there, Miss Cara," Mr. Snyder said as I came in through the bell-jangling door.

I waved hello and set about finding the items on my shopping list. They had everything I needed except for a basket. They even had a starter cake-decorating set that I could use for the name cookies. Luckily, Bubbe had supplied all the other kitchenware I'd need.

At the checkout counter, Mr. Snyder carefully placed my groceries in a paper sack. "Looks like someone's going to be doing some baking," he said.

"Yes, sir," I said. "At least, I'm going to try."

"Well, like I always say, successful baking comes from the heart. You have to love what you're baking to bring it to life." Mr. Snyder smiled and handed me my groceries.

I thanked him and headed home, hoping he was right and that a little love would bring Mom's cookies to life.

In the apartment, I set up shop. I decided to store all the ingredients in the cabinet above the refrigerator because Dad never went into that one.

I got Mom's recipe for chocolate-chip cookies, took a

deep breath, and turned the oven dial to 350. All at once I felt my whole body tingle. I knew it seemed crazy, but I felt as if Mom were there with me in the kitchen. No, not just in the kitchen, but inside of me, helping me along.

As I started to soften the butter and sift the flour, I realized I knew exactly what I was doing. I had helped Mom make these cookies so many times, I didn't even have to check the recipe. I did, though, because I liked looking at Mom's handwriting and thinking of her carefully writing out these instructions. It was as if she had written a personal letter to me.

"In a medium-sized bowl, sift together the 2½ cups flour with the 1 teaspoon baking soda and 1 teaspoon salt." I remembered Mom explaining the need to sift and not simply scoop or pour. Sifting added air to the flour, and even though you couldn't see it, you needed it there to measure the flour properly.

". . . Beat together the sugars with the softened butter until creamy." Mom had taught me exactly how soft the butter needed to be. If it was too hard, it didn't blend well; too soft, the cookies came out flat. She said to think of the butter as my heart. "Keep it soft to let love in, but don't let it go to mush."

"Add the 2 teaspoons vanilla extract and the 2 eggs . . ." I opened the bottle of vanilla and breathed in the delicious smell that reminded me so much of Mom. I dabbed a bit on my wrist. Had Mom done that, too? Was that why she'd always smelled so good?

"Add the dry ingredients and combine until just blended." Timing was everything here. You couldn't over-mix the dough at this point, or the cookies would be too heavy. I watched carefully and turned the Mixmaster off as soon as the flour disappeared.

After stirring in the chocolate chips, I dropped the spoonfuls of cookie dough evenly on the cookie sheets. I kept the oven light on and watched as the cookie dough spread, then rose, then turned a perfect shade of golden brown. Why I had ever doubted myself? I was a great baker. Mom had told me so dozens of times.

As the cookies cooled on wire racks, I considered biting into one. They looked so perfect and warm and, oh, they smelled so good. Whenever I baked with Mom, I wanted to eat the cookies the minute they came out of the oven, but Mom always said, "Not yet, Cara. It's too soon."

But after the cookies had cooled, I knew I couldn't eat even one. Instead, I placed them in a Ziploc bag and hid them behind a box of Popsicles in the freezer. I opened the windows in the apartment. It was cold, but I needed to get rid of the smell before Dad got home.

While I washed the dishes, I thought about the baby Julia just starting her life. I wished I could cast a spell to make sure nothing bad would ever happen to her or her family, but I knew that was impossible. Life was filled with good and bad, joy and sorrow. That's the world God created. I had a feeling, though, that God was rooting for the good, same as I was.

~ ~ ~

On Friday after school I baked the snickerdoodles and the oatmeal cookies, and figured out the bus route I'd have to take to deliver the basket.

According to the lady on the phone at the bus company, I could pick up the number 4 bus three blocks from my apartment. One transfer and forty-five minutes later, I should be two blocks away from Renee's daughter's house. Yikes! I'd never taken a bus by myself before. What if something went wrong? What if I got lost? Or the bus ran out of gas? Or we crashed? Or I missed my transfer? What if it rained, and the cookies got soaked? Stop, stop, stop, I told myself. I would not worry my life away. Worrying didn't help. Now it felt like wasted energy. Besides, even if everything went wrong, I'd find a way to deliver the cookies.

Hey! Maybe that's what God did. Maybe he helped you figure stuff out for yourself. Even when things got crazy. That made a whole lot more sense to me than a

God who swooped in like a superhero every time I sent
him a worrying message.

~ ~ ~

Saturday night, the Wittenbergs took me to Justin's
game. I didn't know if it was because of the baking, or
my new thoughts about God, or the sound of squeaking
sneakers on the gymnasium floor, but I felt so light, so
free. I whistled and clapped and screamed from the side-
line. Just like before. I almost wished Marlee could see
me.

The next day was February 29, Leap Year Day. As I got
dressed for Sunday school, I thought about how this was
a bonus day, given to us only once every four years. It
seemed like a day made for something special. Maybe a
day to talk to Marlee.

I realized I'd been waiting and waiting for Marlee to
apologize to me, but the truth was, it wasn't all her fault. I
owed her an apology, too. She'd never acted the way my
dad did, and I shouldn't have compared them. I knew it
wasn't fair for me to burden her with my sadness all the
time. I sure didn't like Dad's doing it to me.

I decided to make Marlee a card using my scrapbook
supplies. I folded a piece of yellow paper in half, and I cut
two big circles out of pink and blue paper. I glued the

blue circle to the front of the card and drew a frowny face on it. Then I wrote "I'm blue without you!" Inside, I glued the pink circle onto an accordion-folded strip of paper so it would pop out when Marlee opened the card. I drew a smiley face on the circle and wrote "I'd be tickled pink if we could make up! I'm sorry, Marlee. Love, Cara."

At Sunday school, I tucked the card inside Marlee's Hebrew book when she took a bathroom break. As soon as she came back, she looked at the card, then looked over at me and smiled. She scribbled on the back of the card and held it up to me.

"I'm sorry, too. Friends?"

I wrote, "Absolutely," on my notebook, and showed it to her. We both sighed huge sighs. It sure took a lot of energy to fight with your best friend.

After Sunday school, when we were waiting in the car pool line, I told Marlee I had a big secret.

"What?" she asked.

"Promise you won't tell anyone? Not even Max?"

"Of course, of course! What is it?"

"I've been impersonating my mother."

Marlee squinted at me. "Huh?"

So I explained everything, and she listened with wide eyes and a huge smile.

"So," I said, "the only thing left to do is make the

name cookies, buy a basket, and deliver it all . . . tomorrow. Are you in?"

"Ha! What kind of question is that? You bet I'm in! I can't believe I was out for a whole week!"

Marlee put her arm around me, and my dad pulled up. We had the giggles the whole ride home.

~ ten ~

The reason we didn't have school on Monday was that it was Pulaski Day. Casimir Pulaski was a Polish general who'd fought in the American Revolution, and we got the day off in his honor. But what I wanted to celebrate was my mom's birthday. Weird. She wasn't going to turn forty-three. I wasn't going to make her a present or bring her breakfast in bed.

Before getting out of bed, I looked at her picture. *Happy Birthday, Mom. I hope Janie takes good care of you today.*

I decided to call Bubbe and Zayde right after breakfast. Bubbe answered, but as soon as she heard my voice she had Zayde pick up an extension.

"Oh, Cara, it's so good to talk to you today," Bubbe said. Her voice sounded rough, as if she'd been crying.

"Are you okay, Bubbe?" I asked.

"This is a hard day for all of us," Zayde said gently.

"I know," I agreed.

"Are you and Dad doing anything special today?" Bubbe asked. "Maybe dinner at Mom's favorite restaurant or something?"

"Well, we hadn't talked about it, really," I said. "But it's a good idea. I'll suggest it to Dad."

"Oh, good, love. You do that. It makes me feel better knowing we're all thinking of your mom today, and celebrating her life. You know?"

"Yes, Bubbe, I know."

What I really knew was that I wouldn't suggest going out for dinner. Because Dad wouldn't get home until way past dinnertime.

I hung up the phone feeling sad. Sad for Bubbe and Zayde. Sad for me. But mostly sad for Mom.

Marlee came over, and I tucked my sadness away. It wasn't hard because we started baking, and making sure Marlee didn't mess anything up as we followed the tea cookie recipe took all my attention. Before too long, the cookies were cooling on the counter. Even with Marlee sharing the work, I felt Mom's presence. I just knew she was there.

Finally, the time had come to write "Julia" on the

cookies. I knew exactly what to do. I filled the frosting squirter with pink buttercream frosting.

"You try," I said to Marlee, sliding it across the counter.

Marlee gingerly picked up the frosting squirter. "Are you sure?" she asked.

"Yes," I said. "I need your help."

She started in on the first cookie, sticking her tongue out of the side of her mouth as she concentrated. In perfect print letters, she spelled out J-U-L-I-A. Then she smiled. "There."

I examined the cookie. "It's good," I admitted. "But my mom always wrote the names in cursive, not print."

"So?"

"So, you printed."

"So?"

"So, it's not the same." Sometimes Marlee could be so dense.

"But what difference does it make? This looks good. Who cares if it's not exactly the way your mom did it? They're *your* cookies now."

My cookies? I turned that thought over in my head. "You think?"

"Yeah. Well, maybe they're *our* cookies. After all, I *am* the one with the nice handwriting."

I laughed. I let Marlee finish decorating the rest of

the tea cookies. Then we ran to Walgreens to get a basket, some cellophane, and tissue paper, which I paid for with saved-up allowance. My cookies. The more I thought about it, the more I liked the sound of it.

On our way back to the apartment, I collected the mail. There was a package. For me! I looked at the return address and saw it was from Roz.

"What do you think it is?" Marlee asked.

The small brown package was medium weight and about the size of a CD case. "I have no idea."

We rushed upstairs and opened it. Inside was a silver bracelet with the words "Life is a journey, not a destination!" engraved on the top and "Enjoy the moments!" underneath. I'd seen Roz wear it before.

"Cool!" Marlee said.

There was a note:

Dear Cara,

In honor of your mom's birthday, I'm sending you this bracelet. You may remember I have one just like it. Your mom gave it to me when I first moved out to L.A., and it has inspired me many times over the years. You're on your own journey now, a journey you never planned, but still, your own unique path. Enjoy the moments!

Lots of love,

Roz

Marlee read over my shoulder. "When's your mom's birthday?"

"Today."

"Oh, Cara, I'm sorry." She put her arm around me and gave a tight squeeze.

"Thanks," I said, glad that Marlee understood.

"It's kind of cool, though," Marlee said, "that we put this basket together on her birthday. Do you think she knows?"

"Oh, she knows."

"You sound so sure."

"I am. I can't explain it, but I am."

Marlee grinned. "Well, good. Then I'm sure, too."

I slid the bracelet onto my wrist and ran my fingers over the engraved words. I loved it. I had been meaning to call Roz for some time now. I would do it tonight.

Marlee and I put the basket together, cushioning the cookies in colorful tissue paper. But just as I was about to tie off the cellophane wrapping, Marlee said, "Wait! We forgot something."

"Huh?"

"The quote. The little saying. Like Roz said at the funeral. Your mom always put one in each basket."

How could I have forgotten that? Of course. But what would we say? Marlee and I started throwing ideas around.

"Welcome to the world?"

"Girls rule and boys drool?"

"Sugar and spice and everything nice?"

"Girls rock?"

Nothing we thought of sounded good to both of us. Finally, I said, "Let's look in my scrapbook. Maybe we'll see something there."

We paged through the book, studying the photos as we went. At last we found it. The perfect quote. It was from one of the pages I'd taken out of Janie's journal. Marlee wrote it in her best handwriting with little hearts and swirls around the edges. I had to laugh, thinking of how out of context the quote was. Janie had been talking about the start of the soccer season. "Ready or not . . . here I am! A girl like nobody you've ever seen before!"

The basket was complete. The sky was clear blue. I didn't have to worry about rain, after all.

And my worries about taking the bus? A complete waste of energy. It was as easy as the lady at the bus company had said it would be.

Marlee and I stood in front of 1414 Baer Avenue, a small green house with white shutters. My heart pounded so loudly, we probably didn't need to ring the doorbell. But we did, and a second later the door opened.

I held the basket out in front of me, but all of a sudden I couldn't speak. The lady who answered the door must have been Renee's daughter. She seemed to be the right age, and she held a tiny baby in her arms.

"Can I help you?" she asked.

"Uh . . . uh . . ." I stammered.

"Delivery. From Julia's Kitchen!" Marlee said.

"Mom!" Renee's daughter called into the house. "Do you know about a delivery from Julia's Kitchen?"

I couldn't take my eyes off the baby. Little wisps of blond hair framed her pudgy face, and her eyes were steel blue-gray. She looked so content in her mom's arms. So cuddly and sweet. I thought about God. He must have helped create her. I realized that's another thing he does—he helps make babies.

Just then Renee walked up to the door, wiping her hands on a dish towel. She had a huge smile on her face, and she opened the door wider, saying, "Come in, come in. Let me see that basket."

Renee took the basket from me, and we stepped into the foyer. "Mmm, mmm. They smell delicious," she said.

Renee and her daughter looked into the basket.

"Oh, look at those cute cookies with your name on them," the daughter cooed to Julia. "Mom, did you order this? How sweet."

Renee smiled even wider.

Looking at the three of them together—Renee, her daughter, and the baby, Julia—reminded me of a fairy-tale storybook. I felt an ache in my heart. I missed Mom and Janie. I would always miss them.

Renee handed Marlee two twenty-dollar bills and said

to both of us, "Thank you so much for delivering the basket. You can keep the change. And please tell Julia it looks great."

How I wished I could do exactly that. "Thanks," I said. "We will."

I didn't say much on the bus ride home. I felt let down after all the excitement. I thought about Mom and Janie. Marlee tried to talk about what we could do with the forty dollars. She wanted to spend it on music and scrapbook supplies. I couldn't even think about spending the money yet.

Marlee got off the bus close to her home, and I got off near mine. As I opened the door to the apartment, I heard the phone ringing. I figured it was Marlee, calling to make sure I was okay.

"Hello?" I said.

"Hello?" said a voice I didn't recognize. "Is this Julia's Kitchen?"

I took in a sharp breath.

"Yes," I said. "How may I help you?"

~ eleven ~

That's how Marlee and I got into the cookie business.

When people called for Julia's Kitchen, I didn't tell them they had the wrong number or that Julia's Kitchen was no longer in business. I took their orders. We delivered a couple of baskets each week, and the orders kept coming.

We told Mrs. Rosen it was easier to do our homework at the apartment, away from Max and his friends. Mrs. Rosen wasn't wild about us spending so much time unsupervised, but Marlee reminded her that we were eleven, going on twelve. Soon we'd be able to baby-sit. We were certainly capable of hanging out by ourselves for a few hours every day.

And we did do our homework. Quickly. Because as soon as we finished it, we baked, or packaged, or delivered baskets for Julia's Kitchen. We made some serious money, too. We took in about $60 a week. After paying for supplies, we split our profits fifty-fifty. Marlee loved counting the money. And she loved spending her share. She bought tons of scrapbook supplies. I saved mine. I didn't want to spend it on just anything. I wanted to use it for something special, something meaningful. I wondered if there was some way the money could honor Mom and Janie's memory. For now I hid it all in Mom's jewelry box.

Dad didn't have a clue what we were up to. I made sure by buying a few super-sized boxes of Popsicles. I threw out the Popsicles and used the empty boxes to store the cookies. Since Dad hated icy treats, I knew the cookies were safe. And I didn't have to worry about Dad picking up a phone call for Julia's Kitchen because he was never home during the day, when those calls came in.

I still wished Dad and I could have a better relationship, but I didn't think about it every day anymore. Nana would call sometimes and tell me how worried she and Papa were about him, and that would remind me of how things were. But then I would look at my bracelet and tell myself this was my journey. This was my path. Dad's spending all his time working or watching TV was simply part of my journey. If his own mother couldn't help, there was nothing I could do about it, just as there was nothing I could do about finding out what had really happened in the fire.

I was coping, and lately I hadn't even had much to say to Mrs. Block in our weekly sessions.

~ ~ ~

On the first of April, a Thursday, a storm woke me with blasts of thunder. The rain came down in sheets. The sky was dreary gray, lit only by flashes of lightning. It rained like that all day.

After school, Marlee and I raced to my apartment. The wind snapped our umbrellas inside out the minute we walked outside. So we ran and laughed the whole way home, getting soaked. When we reached the building, we looked as if we'd been swimming in our clothes. We were completely drenched, and I, for one, was frozen.

I stood under a small overhang by the front door, looking for my key, while Marlee danced in the rain, her arms raised and her mouth open in a wide grin. "I'm singin' in the rain," she sang, splashing in the puddles.

"You're crazy!" I said. I finally found my key in the bottom of my backpack, but my hands were shaking and slippery from the cold rain, and I dropped the key in a puddle. Just as I reached down to get it, I noticed a cat, shivering next to the wall.

It was him! The Sport look-alike. The one I thought I'd imagined all those weeks ago.

"Marlee, look!"

Marlee stopped her song-and-dance routine and saw where I pointed. "Oh! The poor thing," she said, leaning down to pet him.

"Don't scare him away," I said. But already I could see the cat wasn't going anywhere. He nuzzled his head into Marlee's hands. I opened the door as fast as I could, and Marlee picked the cat up and brought him into the warm safety of the apartment building lobby.

"That's the cat I told you about. Remember?" I couldn't believe he was real. And right here! As if he'd been waiting for me.

"The one that cried outside your door?"

I nodded and moved closer to pet the cat. He purred softly in Marlee's arms. I rubbed under his chin, and he stretched his neck up, loving my touch.

"I wonder where he's been," Marlee said. "He doesn't have a collar."

"I don't know, but he's mine now. I'm adopting him."

"Really? But what if he belongs to someone?"

"Look at him," I said. "He's skin and bones. I'm telling you, this is a stray." I took the cat out of Marlee's arms and held him so I could stare into his eyes. They were pale green with specks of gold. Maybe I'd name him Goldie. Or Rain.

We went up to the apartment and changed our clothes. I tried to dry the cat off with a towel, but he preferred to sit by a warm air vent and lick himself clean. I opened a can of tuna, spooned it into a bowl, and placed it on the kitchen floor along with a dish of water. The cat sauntered over and ate as if he had always lived here.

"Now, don't get used to tuna, little guy," I said. "Tomorrow I'll get some regular cat food at Snyder's."

The cat looked up at me and sneezed.

"You should name him Sneezy," Marlee said.

"I was thinking Goldie or Rain."

"How about Cookie?"

"Too girly. He's a boy cat," I said.

"Well, Goldie's kind of girly, too."

Lightning flashed outside. A second later, thunder crashed, and the cat jumped straight in the air, hair standing on end.

Marlee and I laughed, and at the same moment we both said, "Thunder!"

The cat had a name. He dashed under the sofa and curled up in a ball. Marlee and I lay down on the floor, peeking in at him. He stared back, eyes glowing.

"It's okay, Thunder. It's just a big noise," I said softly.

Thunder stared at me, blinked twice, then closed his eyes and went to sleep.

"You have a cat," Marlee said.

"Yeah," I said, feeling warm all over. "I guess I do."

Marlee and I spent the rest of the afternoon baking. I wanted to stock the freezer with lots of different cookies so we'd be ready for any order that came in.

At six o'clock, I figured it was just about time to clean up. Marlee was pouring brownie batter into a pan. A batch of peanut-butter cookies was almost ready to come out of the oven. I was washing the bowl that I'd used to mix the cookie dough. And Thunder had repositioned himself on a kitchen chair closer to the heat of the oven.

At that moment, the apartment door opened and Dad walked in.

My heart jumped into my throat.

"Mr. Segal!" Marlee said, running to the archway that separated the kitchen from the rest of the apartment. She spread her arms out wide, trying to prevent Dad from seeing into the kitchen. "What are you doing here?"

I stood at the sink, staring at Dad. There was no way to hide what we were doing. Dad could see and smell everything. Pots and pans. Measuring cups. Flour. Sugar. Baskets lined with cellophane. And the smell. That sweet smell I had been so careful to get rid of every other time we had baked—it wafted through the apartment, giving away all our secrets.

"I live here," Dad said, answering Marlee's question in

a monotone voice. "The bigger question is what are you two doing here?"

I felt trapped and defenseless. Yet, I had to admit, I felt something else, too—relief.

"Oh, that's easy to explain," Marlee said, talking fast. "You see, there's this big bake sale at school, and not everyone could make something, so Cara and I volunteered, and we got started baking, and—well, it's not like we bake all the time or anything—it's just for this bake sale. You know, we're raising money to save the, uh, rain forest? Yeah, the rain forest, that's what the bake sale is for, and so—"

"Marlee, stop," I said.

Marlee's mouth hung open. Dad looked at me. I felt Mom inside of me, like an electric current pumping through my veins. I didn't know how Dad would react, but I was ready for anything. I was tired of keeping secrets. And I was tired of not knowing his. I took a deep breath. "Dad, Marlee and I have been keeping Julia's Kitchen alive. That's why we're baking."

Dad looked stunned, as if he'd been slapped. He walked past Marlee into the kitchen and sat down at the table, his coat still on and dripping wet. Marlee looked from me to my dad and back again.

"How long?" he asked.

"For about five weeks," I said. I didn't smile, even though I felt like it. I was proud of myself. But I didn't want to push it with Dad. I wasn't sure what he was thinking. I could tell he was trying to figure it all out.

Just then the oven timer buzzed, and I calmly took the cookies out of the oven. I felt Dad's eyes on me the whole time.

Dad must have realized he was still wearing his coat, so he took it off and laid it across another kitchen chair—the one Thunder was sitting on. Thunder hissed and bolted from under Dad's wet coat, dashing for the safety of the sofa. Dad jumped up from his chair in surprise. "What was that?"

Shoot! That was not how I wanted to introduce Thunder to Dad. But maybe Thunder would take his mind off the baking.

"That's . . . uh . . . Thunder," I said. Then, quickly, "Can we keep him?"

Dad looked around the apartment, as if making sure he had entered the right unit. Then he shook his head, cleared his throat, and said in a calm and sure voice, "No, we can't keep him."

"What do you mean?" I yelled. "Why not?"

"No cats. Not anymore." Dad's voice started to break.

"That's so unfair!" I clenched my fists at my side. Tears welled in my eyes. Why couldn't I have a cat? What was the big deal? Would he make me stop baking, too? He couldn't.

"Marlee," Dad said, "I think you need to go home. Cara and I have some things to discuss."

Things to discuss? My heart pounded with anger. He couldn't just show up and start acting like a real dad—making rules, punishing me. Not without telling me his secret. Not without explaining the fire. I wouldn't let him. It wasn't fair. I ran to my room and slammed the door.

I buried my face in my pillow and planned to stay there forever. I heard Marlee call her Mom. I heard her leave.

Then I heard a knock on my bedroom door.

Dad opened the door.

"Go away!" I shouted, my face still buried in the pillow.

I refused to look up. I figured he would stand there for a minute, not knowing what to do, then he would leave. Tomorrow he would change his mind, let me keep Thunder, and everything would be fine. He'd go back to his life, and I'd go back to mine. But at least I'd have a cat to love.

"No, Cara. I'm not going away this time." Dad's firm voice interrupted my thoughts. He sat on the edge of my bed, not saying anything for about a minute. I would wait him out. I wouldn't talk. I concentrated on breathing. In and out. In and out. Another minute passed. And another. He didn't leave.

I rolled over and propped myself up on my elbow. "What do you want?"

Dad didn't react to my attitude. He kept his voice soft and said, "Cara, please, I know I haven't been much of a father to you lately. I told myself you were okay. You were doing all right at school, and you had the Rosens, and I thought that was enough. I thought you were okay without me. But obviously I made a mistake."

I sat straight up. "No, you didn't. I *am* okay. I don't need you anymore."

Dad's face crumpled, but I didn't care. I wanted to hurt him.

"Besides, if Janie were still alive, and I had died in the fire, you'd have done everything you could to be the best father possible."

"Cara!"

"It's true. You always loved Janie more than me." My words were like knives, and I hurled them at him. The rest of my thoughts came out of my mouth so fast they ran together.

"Janie was perfect in your eyes. She was funny and athletic, and adventurous. And I was just a worrywart who wanted things safe and predictable. And now, now I finally did something risky—I brought back Julia's Kitchen—and you want to take it away from me."

Dad put his hand up like a stop sign. "Whoa, Cara. I never said that."

"But you will. I know it."

"No, Cara. I won't."

I sat there, breathing hard, letting his words sink in.

"Cara, I'm not happy you had to keep this a secret from me, but I think I understand why you did. I'm glad you're baking."

"Glad?"

"Yes." Dad smiled. "And surprised. And, actually, impressed."

I didn't know what to say. I thought I might cry.

"But then why did you send Marlee home?"

"Because Marlee's not my daughter."

I didn't know what to say to that. I felt my heart begin to soften.

"Nana's worried about you," I said.

Dad nodded. "I know. She's been leaving me messages everywhere. But the truth is, I haven't wanted to deal with Nana's strong opinions, even if her heart is in the right place. I've just been really, really sad. And lonely. Can you understand that?"

"Yes." Boy, could I ever.

"Cara, I need to be here for you. We need to be here for each other. These last months, I've been walking around in a stupor, blaming myself for the fire, for losing Mom and Janie, for everything. And meanwhile, I see I've been losing you, too."

Thunder chose that moment to saunter into my room

and jump onto my bed. I rubbed his neck. Dad stood and paced the room.

"Dad, I want to know everything about the fire. I need to know. Keeping secrets makes it worse." My words were slow and measured.

Dad ran his fingers through his hair and looked right at me. I held my breath. I had wanted to know what happened that morning for so long. Then I had kind of gotten used to not knowing. Now I was just plain scared.

"Okay," he said. "You're right."

I let out the breath I'd been holding.

Dad sat next to me on the bed. "We were asleep when the smoke detector went off. At first I thought I was dreaming or that it was a false alarm. But Mom shook me, and I realized it was real. There was smoke everywhere. I told Mom to go next door to call 911, and I would get Janie. It was so dark. I had to crawl down the hall to Janie's room. She was sound asleep. You know how she could sleep through anything. I shook her and explained what was happening. I picked her up and tried to carry her down the stairs, but the smoke was thick and I couldn't stand in it. So I put her down and told her to follow me out on her hands and knees. She was so scared, Cara. She begged me to carry her. And to get Sport. But I'm telling you, it was the only way to escape the smoke. We had to crawl down the stairs."

Dad paused. "She was right behind me."

He stopped and closed his eyes. I guessed he was reliving that morning. I wondered if he'd relived it a thousand times by now, and I felt sorry for him in a way I hadn't before. I felt a lump in my throat. I didn't say a word. I just waited for him to go on, bracing myself for the rest of the story. Dad opened his eyes and looked past me, as if he were seeing the images on a screen behind me.

"When I got outside, I saw your mother coming from next door. I went to her, to hug her, but she wasn't looking at me. She seemed to be searching for something, or someone. Then she screamed, 'Where is she?' And I turned around and realized Janie was gone. She'd been right behind me on the stairs. I swear it. But I should have carried her. I should have carried her." Dad's voice broke and his eyes filled with tears. Mine did, too.

Dad was breathing fast now, his words coming out choppy. I got the feeling he needed to tell this story as much as I needed to hear it. And he was going to get to the end no matter how hard it was.

"Mom ran right past me, screaming for Janie. I grabbed her. I tried to stop her. But she was frantic. She twisted out of my arms and ran into the house. I chased after her. I almost ran into the house myself. But right after Mom went in, the fire spread to the front door, and I couldn't get through. It was just a moment, but the whole first floor was engulfed by flames.

"Soon after, I heard sirens, and the firefighters arrived. They attempted a rescue. I waited and waited outside. Praying. Wishing I had carried Janie out, or I had stopped Mom, or I had gone in after them both. And then the firefighters carried them out. And I knew. I knew the minute I saw them in the firefighters' arms. I knew they were gone. They gave them CPR, and they rushed them to the hospital. They worked on them there, too. But it was too late. There was too much smoke."

Dad was sobbing. Hot tears stung my own eyes. I didn't know what to do, so I just hugged him. And we stayed together like that for a long time.

Finally, Dad pulled away. He blew his nose and wiped his eyes. He looked right at me. "They found them together, Cara, in Janie's room. Sport was there, too. They think Janie went back for Sport. She went back to save her cat." Dad looked at Thunder and shook his head.

My mouth hung open. I felt dizzy and sick. No wonder he wouldn't let me keep Thunder.

"I—I didn't know," I said.

Dad nodded. "That's my fault. I'm sorry. I am so sorry." He said each word as if it weighed a hundred pounds.

Tears streamed down my face.

Dad handed me a tissue. Then he went to my dresser and looked at my scrapbook. It was open to the page I had made of Mom and Janie. He studied it, then turned to me. "You are so much like your mother, Cara." He shook his head.

"I know, I'm sorry."

Dad scrunched his eyebrows together, obviously not understanding.

"I'm sorry that I remind you of Mom," I explained.

"Oh, Cara, no. You're a beautiful reminder. I loved her. More than you know. And I love you, too. Always have."

I bit my lip and stared at Dad, this new dad, this old dad, my father.

"Listen, Cara. I know you're not Janie," he said. "Janie was Janie. I love you for being you. For being serious and quiet and careful. I even love you for being stubborn and independent and sneaky, too."

I had been pretty sneaky these last five weeks. But now I wouldn't have to.

"I didn't really like sneaking around with the baking," I admitted. "It's just that I didn't know how you would react. And I wanted to do it for me. It helped me feel close to Mom. It helped me move on."

Dad nodded. "I can tell."

"So what do we do now?" I asked.

"Well, for starters, I can cut back on my hours. I can try to be here for dinner from now on."

"Really?"

"Yeah, and maybe I can help out with Julia's Kitchen."

"Dad, you don't bake," I said, picturing Dad in an apron.

"No, but you're going to have to advertise if you want to be a success, right? I know a little about that."

Dad grabbed a pencil and a notebook and started sketching ad ideas. "We could do flyers, hit the local paper. That shouldn't cost too much. What do you think?"

I smiled through my tears. "I think it sounds great, Dad. Great."

~ twelve ~

The next morning, the sun streamed in through the slats of my mini-blinds. I opened my bedroom window and breathed in that fresh after-rain smell. The streets were wet, and trees dripped water when the wind blew. The storm had passed.

I went to the kitchen and found Thunder standing by his empty bowl, looking up at me expectantly with his cute brown-and-white face. Oh, how I wished I could keep him. I sat for a minute on the kitchen floor, petting his soft, silky fur. I thought about begging Dad one more time, promising him I would never risk my life to save a cat. But I knew it was more than that. Just having a cat around would remind Dad every minute of that horrible day and of Janie's mistake.

"What am I going to do with you?" I asked Thunder. He purred and flopped over for a belly rub.

I couldn't give him to Marlee because of her mom's allergies. And no way would I take him to the animal shelter. They kill cats who don't get adopted quickly enough there. I could put up signs and find a good family for him. Or maybe . . . maybe I already knew a good family—Justin's. They had taken care of Sport when we went to Florida. Maybe they would take Thunder. It was worth a try.

I fed Thunder and was about to get myself some Frosted Flakes when I noticed a note taped to the cereal box. "Cara, Have a grreat day. Love, Dad." He was being funny. Making a joke of Tony the Tiger. Not such a great joke, but still. At least he was trying. I took the note and tucked it carefully into my scrapbook. I would glue it in later.

I poured the cereal, but then I changed my mind. The peanut-butter cookies Marlee and I'd made yesterday sat on the counter, tempting me. I remembered the day of the funeral, when I'd sworn not to eat another dessert again. I'd thought then that Mom would never bake with me, but I was wrong. Mom was with me all the time. Not in a way I could see or touch. But in a way I could feel. In my heart. And just like that, I knew it was time. I stuck two cookies in the microwave for seven seconds, just enough to warm and soften them. I poured myself a tall glass of milk. Then I sat at the kitchen table and took a bite.

Oh, delicious! Nutty, and buttery, and sweet. The cookie melted in my mouth, and the cold milk washed it down perfectly. A little piece of heaven. *Thanks, Mom!*

As I ate the cookies, my mind started spinning. I needed to take care of Thunder. And talking to Dad last night had helped me figure out how I could honor Mom and Janie's memory with the money from Julia's Kitchen. I could give it to the fire department, and they could use it for safety education. Plus, it was Friday—tonight was Shabbat. Mom had always made sure our Shabbat dinners were extra special when we were celebrating something— a birthday, their anniversary, the end of the school year, whatever. I felt that Dad and I had something to celebrate, too. A new beginning.

So after I finished eating the cookies, I called Bubbe.

"Hello?"

"Hi, Bubbe."

"Well, good morning, love! How are you, Cara, dear?"

"I'm good. But I need your help with something."

"Oh? What can I do for you, sweetheart?"

"Well . . . I want to bake Mom's challah."

"That's terrific. Zayde and I were just talking about

planning a trip to see you this summer. We can do it then."

"But, Bubbe . . . I want to bake it today, after school. I need to bake it today."

"Oh . . ." Bubbe said, and silence filled the air. I pictured her on the other end of the line. Was she sitting down in her yellow kitchen? Or was she in the beige living room with her bright paintings covering the walls?

I had looked at Mom's challah recipe dozens of times before, but unlike her other recipes, this one was extremely vague. One part said, "Add 9 to 11 cups of flour slowly until dough forms ball and bounces back at touch." There was a huge difference between 9 cups of flour and 11. How was I supposed to know what kind of ball it should form? Or how bouncy it should be? The recipe was just a sketch. If only I had made the dough with Mom. Instead, I would have to rely on Bubbe.

Thankfully, Bubbe didn't ask me why it had to be today. She didn't tell me baking challah was too hard to explain over the phone or that she'd have to call me after her hair appointment, or golf game, or anything.

She simply said, "I see . . . Well, in that case, let's start from the beginning."

She was a good teacher. I scribbled detailed notes on the back of Mom's recipe. And during our conversation, I filled her in on Julia's Kitchen and things with Dad. It was so easy to talk to Bubbe. I had forgotten how good it could feel. Before we hung up, I promised her I'd call more often. And I meant it.

I glanced at the clock and saw I'd be late for school. So I ran out the door, promising Thunder I'd introduce him to his new family later that afternoon.

At school I told Marlee everything that had happened after she left yesterday. She was as excited for me as I was. But she was really sad about Thunder.

"Are you absolutely, positively sure there is no way you can keep him?"

"Absolutely," I said. "Even if Dad said yes, I couldn't do that to him. But I'm going to see if the Wittenbergs will adopt Thunder."

A smile spread across Marlee's face. "Oh, that's a good idea. Janie would like that."

As soon as I got home, I made the challah dough. It would need to rise for an hour before I could braid it, so I emptied everything out of my backpack and put Thunder inside, leaving it unzipped just enough for him to stick his head out if he wanted.

I slipped my backpack over my chest so the pouch faced forward, and I headed outside. The fresh cool air blew across my cheeks as I strode off toward the bus stop. Taking a bus wasn't scary at all for me anymore. Thunder poked his head out of the backpack, and I pretended I was a mom carrying my baby in one of those baby-sling-thingies.

The number 4 bus let me off at the corner of my old street. My house stood, boarded up and lonely, with a FOR SALE sign out front. I supposed someone would buy it, knock it down, and build something new. "What do you think, Thunder? Should we try to look inside?"

Thunder didn't respond.

"You're no help," I said.

I stared at the house. If I went inside, would all my good memories of our home before the fire be erased by what I saw? Or would I maybe find something important—something Dad missed when he was here last time? I decided I had to know. I made my legs walk in the direction of the house even as my brain was telling me to stop.

I stepped over the sagging yellow caution tape, my heart pounding. I pushed on the wooden board that had replaced our front door. It didn't budge. I pushed harder. I kicked it. Then I noticed it was nailed to the doorframe. I walked around the house, but the back door and all the windows were boarded up, too. Maybe it was meant to be this way, I decided. Maybe it was better not to go inside.

I started back toward the front of the house, but out of the corner of my eye, I noticed something—a small hole in one of the boarded-up windows. I ran to the window and stood on my tiptoes. I peered through the hole. Nothing. I saw nothing. It was too dark. Even though I knew I was looking at the family room, I couldn't see a thing.

So I walked away. And I remembered our family room. I remembered playing games, watching movies, just hanging out together. "We had a lot of fun there, Thunder," I said. "You would have loved it."

I walked five houses down, to Justin's house, and I rang the bell.

"Hi!" I said when Justin answered the door.

"Hey, Cara. What are you doing here?"

"Well," I said, smiling proudly, "I have a surprise for you." I stepped inside, reached into my backpack, and lifted up Thunder.

Justin's eyes opened wide. "Is that Sport?" he asked in a whisper.

I shook my head. "No, this is Thunder, Sport's long-lost twin." I put Thunder in Justin's arms, and Justin smiled, showing off new braces.

"Janie would have wanted you to have him."

"What do you mean?" Justin tilted his head.

Just then Mr. Wittenberg came to the front hall. "Cara, what's this?"

"It's a stray cat—Thunder. I found him, but I can't keep him. And I thought Justin might want him. If it's okay with you."

Justin looked up at his dad, reminding me of Janie that day at the animal shelter. "Please, Dad? Please?"

Mr. Wittenberg screwed up his face. "A cat? Are you sure?"

"Not just any cat, Dad! It's Sport's long-lost twin!"

Mr. Wittenberg looked at me. He looked at Justin. He looked at Thunder. Then he reached out and rubbed Thunder's head. "I can't believe I'm saying this, but I've always been a softie for pleading eyes, and I see three sets of them right here. Okay, Justin. You can keep the cat. But he's going to be your responsibility."

"Yes!" Justin said. "My own cat!"

I let out a big sigh, feeling happy and sad all at once.

"Do you want to stay for a while, Cara?" Mr. Wittenberg asked.

"I can't today, I'm kind of in a rush. But I'll come by another day. Take good care of Thunder!"

I dashed to the bus stop and got there just as the number 4 pulled up, and I hopped on board.

Back at the apartment, I was greeted by the sweet smell of rising challah dough, reminding me of home, Mom, and family Shabbat dinners. The dough had doubled in size, and it was time to punch it down and braid it. I sprinkled a big board with flour and gently eased the dough out of the bowl and onto the board. Then I punched it, *wham!* My fist left a big depression in the middle, but the dough began to spring back. I kneaded it for a few minutes, loving the feel of dough in my hands. I divided the dough into three sections for three challah loaves, two for Shabbat and one for the freezer. Then I divided each section into nine pieces, rolled them into long snakes, and braided them. Beautiful. I set the three braided challot on the counter to rise again. I would have just enough time for my last errand.

I went to my room and counted out my money from Julia's Kitchen. I had $95! I put the money in an envelope and stuck it in my pocket. Then I headed to the Walden fire station. I walked up the steps to the brown brick building and through the front door. A round-faced woman with short black hair sat behind the front desk and hung up the phone as I approached. "Can I help you with something?" she asked, smiling.

"Um . . ." I said, not nearly as sure of myself as I wanted to be. "Is there someone here who takes donations?"

"What kind of donation?"

"The—um—money kind?"

She laughed, and I felt heat rush to my face.

"Why don't you take a seat, honey, and I'll have the chief out in a minute."

I turned around and sat in one of the gray plastic chairs lining the walls of the small waiting room. Suddenly I wondered if this was a good idea.

It wasn't as if I was simply putting a dollar in the tzedakah jar at Hebrew school or raising money as part of a school effort. This was my personal money, and I was handing it over . . . personally. What if they didn't want it? What if I had to fill out all kinds of paperwork? What if the money just sat and sat and never got used? Or what if it got used for something totally stupid?

And then the worst thought of all occurred. What if they made a big deal out of it and called the newspaper and I got plastered all over the place as a goody-goody? I could just imagine the headline: *Girl Loses Mother and Sister in Fire; Donates Life Savings to Fire Department.* Ugh!

I got up to leave. I would mail in my donation anonymously with a note about how to use the money. But just then, a tall African American man wearing black slacks and a white button-down shirt came into the foyer.

"Sorry for the wait, young lady. I'm Chief Peterson," he said, shaking my hand. He looked at me closely. "And you're . . . Cara Segal, right?"

"Yes, but—how did you know?"

"Come into my office," he said, putting his hand on my shoulder and leading the way.

I was stuck. His office was a small wood-paneled room with one window, a desk, and two chairs. There were papers all over the desk and plaques all over the walls. I sat down, clutching my envelope, trying to figure out how he knew my name.

Chief Peterson looked at me for a while before he spoke. Then he said, "I'm so sorry for your loss."

I opened my mouth. Closed it again. Shifted in my seat.

"I was at the hospital." He paused and looked down at his desk. "And at the fire."

So that was it. He must have been one of the firefighters who had tried to save Mom and Janie.

"It was a terrible tragedy," he said, shaking his head. "How are you and your dad holding up?"

"We're doing . . . okay," I said. And then, trusting him, I said, "I wanted to make a donation to the fire station. I was hoping this money could go toward education. So that people would know things like you shouldn't leave your toaster oven plugged in, and you shouldn't try to save your pets, and—and—"

"And you shouldn't ever run back inside a burning building," he said, finishing my sentence for me.

I looked at Chief Peterson's brave, serious face, and I knew he understood. I nodded, relieved.

I knew he would use this money well. He would do whatever he could to prevent another tragedy like ours. And I knew now that people prevented most tragedies— not God. It wasn't as if I was letting God off the hook, though. It's that I realized God works his magic by giving us the strength to handle just about anything that comes our way. And for what we can't handle alone, he gives us friends and family.

I handed Chief Peterson the envelope, then checked my watch. I had to hurry home. Dad would be there, and the challot were ready to go into the oven.

~ Glossary ~

Bar Mitzvah: At age thirteen, a Jewish boy is considered mature enough to be responsible for fulfilling religious law. To commemorate this growth, the boy is called to the Torah (a scroll of parchment containing the first five books of the Hebrew Scriptures) to recite blessings and to lead the congregation in prayer. Parents express their joy at this time in their child's life by throwing a party. Both the boy and the party are called a Bar Mitzvah.

Bat Mitzvah: At age twelve, Jewish girls are considered mature enough to be responsible for fulfilling religious law. However, many Jewish girls today wait until age thirteen to celebrate becoming a Bat Mitzvah.

challah: braided bread eaten on Shabbat and other holidays

challot: plural form of challah

keriah: the act of ripping a garment or a black ribbon as a sign of grief

kiddush: prayer said over a cup of wine or grape juice to sanctify Shabbat and other holidays

kugel: casserole dish or baked dessert

mezuzah: case affixed to the right side of the doorways of Jewish homes, containing a small portion of Deuteronomy handwritten on parchment

mezuzot: plural form of *mezuzah*

motzi: blessing over bread

mourner's kaddish: prayer of comfort for the soul of the departed, recited by mourners after the death of a loved one

Shabbat: the Jewish Sabbath, or day of rest and worship, which begins Friday evening before twilight, when women traditionally light candles, and ends Saturday after sunset

Shabbat Shalom: a greeting that means "Sabbath Peace"

Shema: an important Jewish prayer, which proclaims the belief in one God

shin: twenty-first letter in the Hebrew alphabet, often seen on the outside of mezuzot because it stands for Shaddai, one of God's holy names

shiva: a seven-day mourning period when friends and family visit and comfort mourners

tzedakah: literally means righteousness, justice, or fairness, but is also understood as charity

~ Cara's Chocolate-Chip Coofies ~

2½ cups sifted flour

1 teaspoon baking soda

1 teaspoon salt

1 cup packed light brown sugar

½ cup granulated sugar

2 sticks unsalted butter, softened in microwave for
   20 seconds

2 teaspoons vanilla extract

2 large eggs

12 ounces semisweet chocolate chips

In a medium-sized bowl, sift together the 2½ cups flour with the 1 teaspoon baking soda and 1 teaspoon salt. Stir and set aside. In a large bowl, beat together the sugars with the softened butter until creamy. Add the 2 teaspoons vanilla extract and the 2 eggs. Mix well. Add the dry ingredients and combine until just blended. Stir in the chocolate chips. Preheat oven to 350 degrees. Drop heaping teaspoons of dough onto ungreased cookie sheets and bake for 10 minutes, or until golden brown. Remove cookies onto cooling racks.

Makes approximately 50 cookies

~ Acknowledgments ~

I could never have written this book without the help
of so many people. Kathryn Jensen Pearce at the Institute
of Children's Literature taught and encouraged me from
the beginning. Rachel Glasser and the Sydney Taylor
Manuscript Award committee acknowledged this story
when it was still a work in progress. Carol Grannick and
the other members of our critique group constantly
pushed me to do better. Rabbi Alex Felch of Congregation B'nai Tikvah and Director Keith Patterson of the
Deerfield Fire Department answered all my questions, no
matter how many times I asked the same ones. Julie
Learner gave me valuable insight into the pain and beauty
of grief. And Beverly Reingold made my dream come

true when she said, "Welcome to FSG." Thank you all for the roles you played in bringing *Julia's Kitchen* to life.

A special thank you to Mom and Dad for raising me to believe I could accomplish whatever I set my mind to and to Micky for being the world's best sister and friend. Jacob, Faith, and Sammy, you are delicious. And Alan, how blessed we are! For your love, laughter, and support, I am eternally grateful.